THE LAST COWBOY STANDING

Carla Cassidy

HARLEQUIN®

ROMANTIC SUSPENSE™

ISBN-13: 978-1-335-75951-1

The Last Cowboy Standing

Copyright © 2021 by Carla Bracale

Harlequin Enterprises ULC
22 Adelaide St. West, 40th Floor
Toronto, Ontario M5H 4E3, Canada
www.Harlequin.com

Printed in U.S.A.

"He told me no matter where I went he would find me. I figured if what he said was true, then I might as well move back here."

Mac frowned. "Do you have any idea who it might be?"

She shook her head. "Not a clue. I never saw him at all and I knew he was disguising his voice every time he talked to me."

"Do you really think he'll come back for you?" His eyes were dark and troubled.

There was no way she was willing to share with him that she hoped the madman would come back for her. She cared about Mac, but she didn't want him to try to play her hero.

She didn't need a hero.

"No, I really don't think he'll come for me again." She hated to lie to Mac, but this was a lie to keep him safe. "I think he was just saying that to scare me. He'd be a fool to try it twice. And now I don't want to talk about any of this anymore. This night was supposed to be a celebration."

* * *

Don't miss the other exciting romances in the Cowboys of Holiday Ranch miniseries!

* * *

If you're on Twitter, tell us what you think of Harlequin Romantic Suspense! #harlequinromsuspense

Dear Reader,

Well, the time has finally come to say goodbye to the twelve boys who came to the Holiday ranch for a second chance at life. They're now all grown up, and each have found that special woman to make their lives complete.

I must confess, I'll miss these guys. They have been a part of my life for some time now. I feel a bit like Big Cass. All I wanted was for these cowboys to find love and happiness, so my job now is done and my heart is full.

Yes, it's time to move on from the Holiday ranch...or is it?

Carla Cassidy

Carla Cassidy is an award-winning, *New York Times* bestselling author who has written over 170 books, including 150 for Harlequin. She has won the Centennial Award from Romance Writers of America. Most recently she won the 2019 Write Touch Readers Award for her Harlequin Intrigue title *Desperate Strangers*. Carla believes the only thing better than curling up with a good book is sitting down at the computer with a good story to write.

Visit the Author Profile page at Harlequin.com for more titles.

Chapter 1

Mac McBride put his horse in the appropriate stall, washed up at the sink in the stables and then headed to the back of the cowboy motel for lunch. The mid-September air was crisp and smelled fresh with just a hint of apples and woodsmoke.

Autumn was one of Mac's favorite times of year and the small town of Bitterroot, Oklahoma, celebrated the season with a big fall festival, which had taken place the week before.

It always seemed like everyone in town came out for the festival. There were tents set up with food for sale and with various craft items. There were all kinds of contests, from bobbing for apples to best-baked apple pies, and a Miss Bitter-root was always crowned.

The theme of the weekend had been fun and family, and as far as Mac was concerned, there was no place in the entire world that did it better than the small town he loved.

He'd come to the Holiday ranch when he'd been a fifteen-year-old off the streets of Oklahoma City. Now, at thirty-six, he figured he'd work there until he got too old to be an asset to the ranch and then buy a small house in town and retire.

There were twelve young boys who had come to the ranch to work and live. Ten of those men were now happily married and one of them was dead. Of the married men, some still worked on the ranch, while others had their own places.

He smelled the scent of barbecue before he walked into the dining area doorway. Cord Cully aka Cookie had been cooking for the cowboys for years. He provided breakfast, lunch and dinner, and he knew what they all liked.

Mac walked inside the dining room and was greeted by several of the other cowboys who were in the buffet line Cookie set up for each meal. "Hey, man," Dusty Crawford said as he fell in line behind Mac.

"Hey, Dusty. I hadn't really congratulated you and Tricia being pregnant again. I heard about it a couple of weeks ago but every time I see you I forget to say something."

Dusty's dimples danced in his cheeks as he grinned at Mac. "Thanks, we're both really happy about it."

"That's great, Dusty." Mac picked up a plate and silverware and moved closer to the food.

"When are we going to get you married off?" Dusty asked teasingly. "You're the last cowboy standing when it comes to love and marriage among us original guys."

"I've pretty much decided that's not in the cards for me," Mac said. "I've made peace with the fact that I'll probably live my life alone. I'm satisfied just working here and playing my guitar when anyone wants to hear me, for as long as I'm able."

"You know the guys always like to hear you strum and sing after a long day," Dusty replied.

Usually during the evenings, some of the men would gather in the rec area on the other side of the dining room and Mac would entertain them with his music. That was what fed his soul.

"I'm starving," Dusty said.

"You're always starving at lunchtime," Mac said with a laugh. "But it's definitely a good food day." This meant pulled pork sandwiches, french fries and coleslaw. There was also baked mac and cheese and fresh fruit.

Mac filled his plate and then went to one of the

picnic tables and slid into an empty seat. Dusty followed and sat across from him.

"I think I've got a new horse to work with in the evenings," Mac said.

"That's cool. Whose?" Dusty asked.

Mac knew what he was about to say would shock Dusty. When Mac had gotten the call the night before, he had been utterly surprised. "Marisa Lindale."

Dusty froze with his sandwich halfway between his plate and his mouth. His blue eyes widened. "Marisa Lindale? Are you kidding me?" He put the sandwich down and stared at Mac in disbelief.

"No, I'm not. She called me last night. I'm meeting with her tonight and looking at the horse she wants me to work with."

Dusty picked up his sandwich again. "I didn't even know she was anywhere here in town. Is she staying out at her mother's place?"

"No, not in the big house itself. Apparently she's been living in a foreman's cabin at the back of her mother's pasture," Mac replied.

Dusty frowned. "What's it been… Two…three years since she was abducted?"

"Almost two years ago. I checked after she called me."

Twenty months ago Marisa Lindale had been

living in Oklahoma City and working for a large company in their tech department.

On that particular night, according to the news stories, she'd made plans to meet some friends at a local bar, but she'd never made it there. She'd disappeared someplace between her apartment and her car in the parking lot, although her purse and her keys were found in the car.

She was missing for sixty days, and had then appeared on the streets of her hometown, Bitterroot, Oklahoma, bound and gagged in front of the post office on Main Street.

It was a huge story when she'd told police she'd been abducted by an unknown man and held captive for two months. Her beautiful face and the lurid tale had been splashed across news stations throughout the country for days. Then she had disappeared completely from the public eye.

Like with most news stories, once she fell off the front pages, people eventually stopped talking about her and the crime, and soon after, everyone forgot about her.

"Man, I wonder how she's doing now," Dusty said. "And I wonder how long she's been living here right under our noses."

"I got the impression after our brief conversation last night that she's been at that foreman's cabin for quite some time," Mac replied.

"She sure has been a recluse," Dusty said. "I've certainly never seen her in town."

"I don't think anyone has," Mac replied.

The conversation then turned to the many things the cowboys needed to get done before winter moved in. Tony Nakni sank onto the bench next to Dusty.

Tony was another one of the original twelve young boys who had arrived on the ranch to work for Big Cass Holiday. He'd married Mary Redwing, a talented local artist, several years ago, and they lived in a house in town with Mary's colorful grandmother, Halena.

"Did you hear that the fence was down in a section of the west side of the pasture this morning?" Tony asked.

Dusty frowned. "I didn't hear anything about it, but I've been mucking out stalls all morning."

"And I was in the stable with Dusty, polishing and oiling all the horse equipment. Did any of the cattle get out?" Mac asked.

"From what Sawyer told me, we're missing five," Tony replied.

Dusty frowned. "And they're probably wearing the Humes brand by now."

Mac sighed. "Things have been so quiet between them and us. I was hoping it would stay that way."

The Humes ranch was next to theirs. It was

owned by Raymond Humes, an old man who had hated Big Cass and now hated her niece Cassie, who had taken over the ranch after Cass's death.

Over the years there had been fires set, cattle stolen and fencing downed on Holiday Ranch, and they knew the Humes men were responsible, although there had been no arrests due to a lack of concrete evidence.

It had to be particularly frustrating to Chief of Police Dillon Bowie, who was married to Cassie. He investigated the crimes taking place on his own property, but was never able to specifically identify the person or persons responsible.

Mac hated to see the mischief and mayhem starting up all over again.

"Those guys on the Humes ranch need to stay in their own lane instead of messing with us," Dusty said with a frown.

"I'd like to catch one of them red-handed when they're cutting our fence so I could give them something to really think about," Tony added gruffly.

"Let's hope this is just an isolated incident and doesn't mean that things are going to get nasty with them again," Mac replied.

The men finished up their lunch and headed back outside for their afternoon chores. Mac returned to the small room in the barn to get back to work oiling and polishing saddles and all the other tack equipment.

This was one of his favorite chores. His first choice would be riding the pasture on the back of his horse, Rachel, named for Mac's mother who had died of breast cancer when Mac was twelve years old. But he enjoyed this work, as well. The smell of the horses and hay and of oil and polish fed his soul almost as much as his music did.

He worked until it was time to knock off for supper. Dusty and Tony went home after work each day, so Mac didn't have them to eat dinner with. However, there were nine others in the dining room and it was usually a raucous meal as they teased each other about the day's work and talked about plans for the coming weekend.

It was a few minutes before six when Mac went to his room and showered up so he could be at Marisa's place by seven. His room was in a long building they all referred to as the cowboy motel. Each man who worked and lived on the property had his own room. The rooms were small but serviceable and each had its own bathroom, as well.

He dressed in a pair of slightly worn, comfortable jeans and a black, long-sleeved turtleneck. He slapped on some cologne, added his cowboy hat and then left his room.

He headed for the large garage in the distance, which housed not only ranch vehicles but also the personal vehicles of all the men who lived on the property. For the first time since that morning, he thought about the meeting he was about to have.

As interested as he was in meeting Marisa Lindale, he was equally interested in the horse he'd be working with. All she'd told him about the mare was that she'd been bought at auction and she needed a lot of work. He would have liked to ask her more questions about the horse, but Marisa had kept the call brief.

He'd just turned onto the main road that would take him to the outskirts of town when he saw flashing red and blue lights in the distance ahead and the light traffic come to a halt.

As he pulled closer, he realized it was a wreck between two vehicles. He hoped nobody was hurt and that the road got cleared quickly.

Right now he was stuck and aware of the clock ticking. He hated to be late, especially on his first meeting with a new client, but there was nothing he could do about it.

It was seven fifteen when the road was finally free and Mac was able to continue on his way. Dusk had already begun to fall and the cloud cover overhead promised a darker-than-usual twilight.

He stepped on the gas, hoping to get there as quickly as possible, while there was still a last gasp of daylight left for him to see the horse.

He turned down the road that would lead him

to the Lindale ranch. Rose Lindale was a widow who owned a big spread. She sat on the city council and was an influential leader in the small town. Currently she was running for mayor of Bitterroot, and local gossip indicated she was probably going to win.

Marisa had told him to go down the driveway along the right side of the two-story Colonial and continue straight ahead. He did that and came to the pasture gate she'd told him about. He got out of his truck and opened the gate. He drove through it and then stopped to close the gate behind him.

He continued on a dirt lane that cut through the pasture and finally saw the small cabin in the distance. No lights shone from the windows and he wondered if, since he was late, she'd left to go someplace else.

As he drew closer he saw the good-sized corral and a shed-like structure connected to it. He parked in front of it and got out of his truck. The tall black mare immediately ran to the opposite side of the corral.

Mac could smell the fear emanating from the undernourished horse as its ears flattened and it cowered away from him. Mac's heart cried out for the pain he sensed the animal carried both physically and mentally.

He leaned forward on the wooden railing. "Hey, girl," he said softly. "Hey, pretty girl. I know you're scared but maybe we can do some things to fix that."

He jerked upright, a small gasp escaping him as the unmistakable feel of a gun barrel jabbed him in the back. "Put your hands up over your head," a low female voice commanded.

Marisa held the gun at the back of the tall man dressed in black. Even though she knew he was probably Mac McBride, she wasn't taking any chances. She hadn't taken a chance with her own safety for the past eighteen months.

"Slowly turn around and keep your hands up," she said.

He did as she asked and she got her first look at the man who would hopefully work with the horse. His light brown hair was slightly shaggy beneath his black cowboy hat and his sculpted features were bronzed from the sun.

But it was his eyes that momentarily gave her pause. Long and dark-lashed, they were chocolate brown, with a wealth of warmth emanating from them. The picture she'd found of him on the internet didn't do him justice, but this was definitely the man she'd been expecting.

"Do you usually shoot people who are late to meet with you?" he asked, his voice holding a touch of humor.

"You can put your hands down now," she replied as she holstered her gun.

He lowered his arms to his sides. "I'm Mac and you must be Marisa," he said.

"I am, and that's Spirit." She pointed to the horse. "I named her that because right now she's broken, but I'm hoping with the right care she'll find her spirit again."

She'd been watching an online auction out of Tulsa and the minute she had seen Spirit, she knew she had to have her...to heal her. She'd known instantly that the horse was destined to be hers.

"What's her story?" Mac once again leaned on the railing and gazed at the horse, who remained on the far side of the corral.

She stepped up next to him and immediately caught his scent, a mixture of sunshine, minty soap and a woodsy cologne that was instantly appealing. "All I know for sure is that she has obviously been underfed and she shows signs of being whipped and beaten."

A rich anger threatened to well up inside her as she thought of the torture the helpless animal had endured.

"Whoever did that to her should be shot," Mac said.

"I share the sentiment," she replied. "I don't even know what or if she had a name before she arrived here. So, what do you think?"

He turned to look at her. He was definitely a piece of rugged eye candy, not that she was interested. "If I decide to take this on, I need you to understand a couple of things." He straightened up, his features getting difficult to read in the darkening evening.

And she positively hated the dark.

"Why don't we go inside and we can discuss this in more detail." Even though she'd had no intention of inviting him into her personal space, she didn't like being out in the dark, where she might be vulnerable to something evil and wicked lurking nearby.

No lights shone from the cabin, but when she opened the front door, the interior of the structure was lit up with a bright ceiling light. The blackout curtains she had hanging on every window kept the lights inside so that nobody would see the illumination from the outside and know the place was occupied.

She only opened the door partway, and instantly her best friend, a German shepherd named Buddy, stood and growled menacingly. "Friend, Buddy," she said firmly. The dog immediately sat and stopped growling.

Marisa turned back to Mac. "Now you can come in."

After he stepped inside she shut and locked the

door behind him. She then turned to watch his face as he took in his surroundings.

"Good-looking dog," he said.

"Don't let his pretty face fool you. If I used the right command and he thought you were a threat to me, he'd rip your throat out."

"Good to know." His gaze swept the room.

Her furnishings were fairly sparse. The living area held a black love seat and a matching chair and desk with her state-of-the-art computer and other equipment. She had paid an arm and a leg to get internet access at the isolated cabin.

The small dinette area held only a wooden table for two that she kept shoved against the wall. Yes, it was simple furnishings but they held a wealth of secrets.

"Please, have a seat," she said and motioned him to the chair.

"It won't be long before you'll need that." He gestured to the stone, woodburning fireplace next to where Buddy sat.

"Don't remind me." She sank down on the love seat, facing him.

"What is your goal for the horse?" he asked.

"I want her to be my horse. I want her to trust and love me and I want to be able to ride her. Now, what are the things you wanted me to understand?"

"First and foremost, this is going to take some

time and a commitment from you to work with me. Second, I never guarantee my results. We could work with her for months and months and never get her to a place where she's the horse you wanted. Some horses are so broken inside they never learn to trust again."

"You definitely have my commitment, and I understand that you can't guarantee anything. I don't care what you charge me. I've done my homework on you and you're one of the best horse whisperers in the whole state."

He winced, the gesture doing nothing to detract from his handsomeness. "I hate that term. It makes it sound like I have some sort of magical powers, and I don't. I'm just a man who loves horses."

"Nevertheless, you're the man I want to work with her. I…I trust you with her." It had been a long time since she'd used the word *trust*. It had been even longer since she'd actually trusted anyone. "Will you work with her?"

"Absolutely," he replied. "In fact, I'm looking forward to it. There's nothing I love better than helping abused horses learn to trust and love again."

For the next few minutes they talked about how and when he would be paid and what hours he would work. "My goal would be to work with the horse every evening after my work day on the Holiday ranch. I also have two days off a week and would like to be here with her at least a couple of hours on those days."

"Surely you need some time off for your social life?" she said.

He grinned at her and an unexpected flash of warmth swept through her from head to toe. He had a beautiful smile. "I don't have much of a social life. Most of the time I prefer to be around horses rather than people."

She couldn't imagine a man who looked like Mac didn't have all the single women in Bitterroot clamoring at his door. However, she didn't care about his personal life. All she wanted from him was his expertise as a horse trainer.

"So we're all set to start work tomorrow evening?" He stood from the chair. "And I promise I won't be late so I don't get a gun in my back again."

Her face warmed as she got up from the love seat. "Sorry about that, but as a single woman living out here all alone, I'm very careful with my security."

"No offense taken." He smiled once again. The gesture didn't just move his mouth; it lit up his eyes and stirred something that had been dormant in her for a very long time.

It wasn't until he was gone that she identified

that something. Attraction. It was a completely unexpected visceral punch to her stomach.

Not that it mattered. The last thing she was looking for in her life was romance. "Don't worry, Buddy. You're the only man I want in my life." His tail thumped the floor and it appeared he grinned at her.

She had gotten Buddy two months after her ordeal had ended. Together they had gone through extensive training to make him not only a friend, but also another weapon in her arsenal.

In the past year Buddy had been her best friend, her support system and her therapist. The dog had been her sanity as she pulled herself out of the nightmare she'd lived for sixty long days.

"Time for the nightly check," she now said to Buddy. Even though she knew nothing had changed in the cabin since the night before, it was a compulsion of hers to make sure before bedtime that everything was still in place.

She lifted up the chair cushion. The sight of the knife and the gun there reassured her. The sofa cushions held another gun and a Taser. Two more Tasers were taped beneath the kitchen table and her computer desk.

Confident that everything was where it was supposed to be, she headed to the small bedroom with Buddy at her heels. The bedroom was just big enough to hold her queen-size bed, one night table and a chest of drawers.

"Good night, Buddy." She pointed to the dog bed at the foot of her bed. The dog gave her a mournful gaze. She ignored him and pulled down the gray spread.

She then changed out of her black jeans and top and into a pair of leggings and a long-sleeved sweatshirt. The fireplace was the only heat source in the cabin and the nights were starting to get very cool. So far she hadn't needed to build a fire, but that time would be approaching quickly.

She got into bed with the lamp on the night-stand lit. She never turned it off. She hadn't slept in the dark since… She didn't want to think about those sixty days. If she put that in her mind before falling asleep she knew her sleep would be filled with horrid nightmares.

She turned over on her side and released a weary sigh. A moment later she felt the bed depress as Buddy jumped up to join her.

She should scold him and send him back to his own bed, but instead she thought about the handsome cowboy who was going to work with Spirit. Mac was the first person she'd invited into her life in almost two years.

Before she had hired Mac, she'd done her research. She knew he was thirty-six years old, had never been married, and lived and worked on the

Holiday ranch. According to her mother, Mac's reputation was impeccable, and her mother's standards were very high.

It didn't matter that Marisa was attracted to him. She'd invited him into her life solely to work with her horse. She was on a mission that she'd prepared for for the past eighteen months.

If all went well, then she was going to get her wish. She was going to kill a man.

Chapter 2

"So, tell us everything," Dusty said at lunch the next day. "What was she like? Was she nice? Was she as pretty as she was when she lived in town before…as pretty as she looked in those newspaper stories about her?"

Mac laughed. "Down, boy. One question at a time."

"Okay, was she as pretty as she looked in the newspaper? As pretty as she was when she lived here in Bitterroot?"

"That's still two questions," Mac said teasingly, and then he sobered. "Those newspaper photos didn't do her justice. She's still very attractive."

Those old photos definitely hadn't captured the beautiful blue-gray of her eyes or the silky shine of her short black hair. They hadn't depicted her clear, smooth complexion or her sultry, full lips.

She was more than pretty—she was drop-dead gorgeous. But there had been a haunting in her eyes, and the energy that had wafted from her was definitely one that would keep most people away.

"What was she like?" Dusty asked.

Mac shrugged. "I don't know, she was like any other woman." There was no way Mac intended to share with Dusty that Marisa had greeted him with a gun to his back. That definitely wasn't normal, especially since she'd been expecting him.

"I'm looking forward to working with her horse," Mac continued. "She looks like she's going to be a real challenge."

Dusty grinned at him and shook his head. "Why do you get more excited about a horse than a pretty woman?"

Mac laughed. "Horses I know. Women I don't."

"I think it's time I was a matchmaker for you again. You definitely need a good woman in your life."

"Please, Dusty. Don't do me any favors. If I remember right, the last time you set me up on a date the woman spent the whole time telling me how much she hated horses."

"How was I to know Marybeth hated horses? I

just knew she was kind of pretty and she was look-ing for a husband," Dusty replied. He looked at Mac seriously. "Don't you want a wife and kids?"

"I've told you before, I just don't think that it's in the cards for me. I'm thirty-six years old, Dusty. If it was going to happen surely it would have hap-pened already. Really, I'm good by myself."

"I'm just so happy in my life with Trisha and the kids. I wish you had the same thing," Dusty replied.

Thankfully, the topic of conversation changed. When lunch ended, Mac headed for the stables and saddled up Rachel. For the afternoon he'd be on horseback, riding the pastures to survey the herd of cattle.

Five men were always riding the pasture to check on the health and welfare of the herd and to make sure no fencing needed repairs. The herd was big and the pastures were vast. But it was the chore Mac enjoyed the most.

As he headed out, he drew in a deep breath of the scent of the cattle and grass and the crisp Sep-tember air. It all smelled like home. "Let's take a ride, Rachel." He patted her neck as she fell into a brisk gait.

The lunchtime conversation with Dusty re-played in his head. There had been a time when Mac had dreamed of a wife, and of babies that he could sing lullabies to before bedtime.

Over the years he had dated a lot, looking for someone who would fulfill all his dreams, but that perfect woman had remained elusive. Finally, about a year ago, he'd just abandoned that dream and made peace with the fact that it just wasn't going to happen for him.

A vision of Marisa Lindale suddenly filled his head. There was no question that she was beautiful. He'd been surprised to experience a swift physical attraction to her, something he hadn't felt toward a woman for a very long time.

When he'd gotten close enough to her, she'd smelled like something dark and mysterious and wildly exotic. It was a fragrance that had enticed him…had somehow called to him.

No matter how drawn he'd initially been to Marisa, ultimately he had a job to do for her and that was it. In any case, she certainly didn't appear like a woman who was open to any kind of social relationship.

The newspaper reports about her time in captivity had been vague, only indicating that she had suffered both mental and physical abuse.

Something like that had to change a person at their very core. He couldn't imagine what she might have suffered at the hands of the abductor. It had to be horrible for her that no arrest had ever happened, that nobody had gone to jail for the crimes against her.

She obviously lived like a hermit, not being seen by anyone in town. He'd noticed the blackout curtains at all her windows. Apparently she didn't want anyone to see the lights outside and know somebody was living in the small cabin.

She was definitely a mystery, but she hadn't hired him to unravel any secrets she might possess. While she had been civil to him, not anything about her had indicated that she'd be open to any kind of a relationship, including just a simple friendship.

His thoughts turned to the horse he would start working with. There was nothing that made Mac angrier than the abuse of a helpless animal. And it was obvious just by looking at her horse that a lot of damage had been done to the poor creature.

Mac hoped he could not only help restore trust in the horse, but also build back the animal's dignity and self-respect.

It was with that thought in mind that after dinner he showered and changed and then headed to Marisa's place. He told himself that the excitement he felt was strictly for working with the mare, but there was no question that Marisa intrigued him, as well.

Unfortunately there was only a couple of hours of sunshine left before night would move in and make it impossible for him to work with Spirit.

At least tomorrow was his day off and he would be able to spend more time at Marisa's.

As he pulled up in front of her corral, her front door opened and she stepped outside. Her black leggings displayed long, shapely legs and the long black sweater hugged her to display curves in all the right places. She also wore a holster with a gun low around her hips and Buddy was at her side.

He shut off his truck engine and stepped out. "Evening, Marisa," he said and then reached back into the vehicle to retrieve his guitar case from the passenger seat. Buddy growled low in his throat, momentarily stopping Mac in his tracks.

"Buddy, chill," she commanded. The dog immediately stopped growling and sat, but he still eyed Mac as if Mac was a tasty treat. "Friend," she said to Buddy.

"Good evening, Mac," she replied and then eyed his guitar case curiously. "What are you going to do with that?"

"I'm going to serenade your horse." He smiled. "It's been not only my own personal experience, but also the word from experts that music can help to soothe a horse."

"Really?" One of her perfectly shaped dark eyebrows quirked upward.

"Really. Horses tend to like classical and country music. I don't know many classical tunes, but I definitely know some country." He grinned again.

"I believe I see your cynicism showing. Just give me time and trust me."

"I can give you all the time you want. Trusting anyone is a process that will need some time," she replied.

For just a moment that haunted look took over her beautiful, long-lashed eyes. For some reason, more than anything Mac wanted to prove that he was somebody she could rely on not only to work with her horse, but also somebody she could depend on in her life.

He scoffed at his own thoughts. Even though he wondered if she needed a friend, she didn't come off as a woman who required anything or anyone. However, he had memories of her being a very socially active person before she'd moved from Bitterroot to Oklahoma City…before her ordeal at the hands of a captor.

He walked to the side of the corral and she fell into step beside him. "For the next couple of days or so what I want to do is just try to calm her," he said. "While she's so afraid and stressed out I can't really begin to do any hands-on work with her."

"That makes sense," she agreed.

He leaned his guitar case against the wooden railing. "I've got a couple of lawn chairs in the back of my truck. Do you plan on sitting outside with me?"

"If it's okay with you," she replied.

"It's more than fine with me. I would prefer that you're with me at all times when I'm working with Spirit. It's vital that she bonds with you. I just hope you don't think I'm shirking my duty by sitting and singing to your horse."

"Since I know nothing about traumatized horses, I'm trusting that there's a method to your madness." A small smile curved her lips. It was there for only a moment and then was gone. "I'll help you with the lawn chairs."

Together they walked to the back of Mac's truck. He was far too conscious of her nearness and her scent, which eddied in the air around him.

She reached in and grabbed one of the chairs and then he lifted out the second one and they headed back to the side of the corral.

They set up the chairs but didn't sit. He leaned against the corral and gestured for her to do the same. Once again Spirit cowered on the opposite side of the corral.

"Hey, sweetheart," Mac said softly. "Hi, Spirit. You are such a pretty girl." Spirit's ears flattened and she took a couple of steps backward. He turned to Marisa. "Now it's your turn to talk to her."

She looked at the horse. "Spirit, I hope we can help you heal up and get strong again. I hope…" She stopped talking and gazed up at Mac. "I don't know what else to say to her."

"It really doesn't matter what you say. You could stand out here and read the newspaper to her. All that's important is that she hears your voice and gets used to it. In fact, I would recommend that during the day you come out to the corral several times and just talk to her."

"Got it," she replied.

He grabbed his guitar case and walked back to the chairs. As he withdrew the musical instrument from inside, she sat in the chair next to his. Buddy sank down in the cool grass next to her.

Mac sat in the other chair with the guitar in his lap and began to strum a country tune. The music filled the quiet of the evening. Spirit's ears perked up.

When the song ended, he immediately launched into another one. There was a stillness, not only in the horse but also in the woman seated next to him.

When he finished the second song, Marisa nodded at him. "You're very good. Have you always played?" she asked.

"Since I was six years old. My mother was big into music. She played the piano and taught me to play, too. Then she started taking me to guitar lessons and I fell in love with the instrument."

"Your mother must be very proud of your talent."

A hard knot of grief twisted in Mac's chest.

"Unfortunately, she passed away from breast cancer when I was twelve years old."

"Oh, I'm so sorry." Her low, silky voice held a surprising depth of sympathy.

He shrugged. "Thanks, but it was a long time ago."

"I lost my father when I was fifteen," she said. This time there was a hint of sadness in her voice.

"I know and I'm sorry for your loss, too," he replied. He vaguely remembered that her father, Jimmy Lindale, had been killed in a car accident.

He began to play another song and for a moment lost himself in memories of his loving mother. She had been his biggest champion and together they had filled the house with music and laughter.

Mac's father had been a relatively distant figure. He was a functioning alcoholic who would come home late every night from his work in a dog food factory smelling of booze. He'd eat his dinner and then go to bed, leaving no time for his son to really bond with him.

But then there were the nights he came home raging at his mother. On those times it wasn't unusual for him to throw his dinner plate against the wall. Mac's mother would send him to his room while his father continued to rage. Still, there was always song and joy when his mother was alive and his father wasn't home.

When Mac's mother had died, all the music and laughter had stopped. Mac mourned not only for her, but also for all that had been lost when she was gone.

He now continued to play until the shadows of night moved in. As darkness approached he sensed a tense energy begin to radiate from Marisa.

He finished playing and then turned to look at her. Her eyes were dark and her features appeared taut. "Are you okay?" he asked.

She looked at him in surprise. "I'm fine." Her eyes deepened in hue as he held her gaze. "I...I just don't like the dark." The confession seemed to come from the very depths of her soul.

"Okay, then we're done for the night," he replied easily. "Tomorrow is my day off and I can come in the morning. How does ten o'clock work for you?"

"Ten is fine." She got up from the chair and folded it up. "If you want, I can store the chairs in the shed so you don't have to carry them back and forth."

"That sounds good," he replied. He put his guitar back in its case and then folded up his chair. He followed her and Buddy to the nearby shed.

She opened the door and immediately flipped on a light. The shed held a single horse's stall, several bales of hay and a little bit of storage space.

She leaned her chair against the wall and then turned to grab his.

He froze and she did the same. Somewhere in the back of his mind he realized he was too close, and he was invading her personal space. He stood near enough to see her dark pupils suddenly expand and hear the swift intake of her breath.

Quickly he took a step back from her. She took the chair from him and he came out of the shed. "Do I need you to let me into the shed in the morning?" he asked as she and the dog walked him toward his truck.

"No, I don't lock it. There's really nothing in there to steal," she replied. "But if you're going to be here in the morning at ten, then don't worry, I'll be ready and waiting for you."

Mac leaned down and picked up his guitar case. "Then I'll just say good-night, Marisa."

"Good night, Mac."

He got inside his truck and watched as the woman and her dog quickly returned to the cabin. For some reason the sight made him a little sad for her. He wondered if she was lonely in what appeared to be her very solitary life.

She didn't like the dark. The truth was she appeared frightened of the night. Entirely understandable, he thought, recalling her captivity and the harrowing time he imagined she'd gone through.

As he drove home he couldn't get her out of his mind. She was worried about her broken horse, but, he couldn't help but wonder, how broken might she be?

Marisa accomplished her evening routine and then changed into her sleeping clothes even though she wasn't a bit sleepy. With Buddy at her side, she stepped out on the back porch and grabbed a couple of logs for the fireplace. Although it wasn't super chilly in the cabin, she just felt like enjoying a fire.

Within minutes she had a roaring fire blazing and a cup of hot chocolate in her hands. Listening to Mac's music this evening had touched her deep in her soul…in a place that had been alive before she had lost all the music, the joy and all the laughter in her life.

She took a sip of the hot drink and thought about Mac. He seemed like a kind, gentle man and yet she somehow felt threatened by him.

Maybe it was because he was really the first man she'd allowed herself to be alone with since a madman had captured her right out of her car in her apartment parking lot in Oklahoma City.

Or maybe he threatened her because she found him very attractive. In another lifetime she might have flirted with him, maybe gone out on a couple of dates with him. Heck, she might have even slept with him if she'd so desired.

But in this place, in this lifetime, she had no interest in developing a relationship of any kind with anyone. She didn't want to do lunch with friends and she wasn't interested in having anything but a professional relationship with Mac.

However, she would do whatever possible to achieve her ultimate goal. For six months after she'd been released, she'd gone to Tulsa, Oklahoma, and had learned how to shoot a gun. She'd taken class after class in martial arts and self-protection and prepared herself mentally and physically for what she wanted most in her life.

Then, a year ago, she'd moved back to Bitter-root and into this cabin. It had been completely easy for her to stay hidden away here. She ordered whatever she needed online and had the items delivered to her mother's house.

She'd been working at a big tech company in Oklahoma City, but she had also developed a healthy business of her own as a web page designer and manager.

After moving to the cabin, she had resumed that line of work; only she now used the name Renee Lane Designs instead of Marisa Lindale Designs. She was slowly building a solid reputation that had her making a nice amount of money per month.

Again her thoughts turned to Mac. There had been a moment in the shed when she'd had an unexpected impulse to reach out and touch his broad chest and to feel the beat of his heart. Maybe it was because somehow her heart had stopped beating in the darkness of those horrendous sixty days, when she'd been locked away by a madman.

Yes, in another lifetime she might have been interested in a man like Mac, but here and now the only things that mattered to her were justice and retribution. And she now felt both mentally and physically prepared for the next step in her personal journey.

She was surprised to awaken the next morning still curled up on the love seat. Buddy slept on the floor nearby and the fireplace held only dying embers that faintly glowed. When she sat up, Buddy got up and stretched.

She slid her legs over the side of the cushions and stood up. "Good morning, Buddy." He ruffed a greeting in return. He followed her to the front door where she let him outside.

While Buddy was doing his morning thing, Marisa got the coffee going. Once she let the dog back inside, she headed for the shower.

The bathroom was small and without a tub to laze in. Maybe before her ordeal she'd been a scented bubble bath kind of person, but now a quick shower to get clean was enough for her.

When she was dressed she went back to the kitchen and poured out kibble for Buddy and then poured herself a cup of coffee. Finally she sank down at the table. Mac would be here in a couple of hours and she was surprised to realize she was looking forward to seeing him and talking to him again.

She didn't know what his music had done for Spirit the night before, but it had momentarily reached in and soothed a rough edge deep inside of her.

As she thought of the day to come, a touch of anxiety welled up inside her. It was an anxiety she expected to nearly choke her by the time early evening arrived.

For the first time since returning here to her hometown, she intended to leave her reclusive lifestyle behind. She planned on having dinner at the Bitterroot Café. Since it was Saturday night she knew the place would be packed. And maybe... just maybe *he* would be there. She was ready to meet again the monster who had destroyed her life...the man who had destroyed her.

At precisely ten o'clock Mac's familiar black truck pulled up next to the corral. She stepped outside with Buddy at her heels. Mac got out of his truck and greeted her with a smile. Oh, he had such a nice smile. It warmed his eyes and invited the recipient of it to trust him...to enjoy life with him.

"It's a beautiful day," he said as he reached in to grab his guitar case.

"It is," she agreed. And he definitely looked hot, clad in a brown-and-red plaid shirt that stretched across his broad shoulders and jeans that fit perfectly on his long, lean legs.

"Friend," she murmured to Buddy and patted his side as he growled at Mac.

Mac laid his guitar case on the ground. "I'll go get our chairs if that's okay with you."

"Sounds perfect," she replied easily. She watched as he walked to the shed. He had a confidence in his gait, as if he was comfortable in his space in the world. Oh, she envied him that. She'd once been comfortable in her own place in life, but now she had no life. It had all been stolen away from her.

Within minutes they were seated side by side. Once again she noticed the scent of him, a pleasant clean smell with a hint of his woodsy cologne.

"Is she eating?" He gestured toward Spirit, who had moved to the back of the corral to eye them warily.

"I never see her eat, but the hay is disappearing as well as the special feed I leave for her."

Mac nodded. "Good. She obviously needs to put on some weight."

"I'm hoping the extra feed will help her fill out," she replied.

He pulled his guitar from the case. "I'll play a little and then we can go into the corral."

"Whatever you say," she replied. "You're the knowledgeable one."

It was pleasant to sit and listen to Mac play his guitar as the sun warmed her shoulders and a light breeze caressed her face. Occasionally she leaned down and petted Buddy, who remained vigilant at her side.

These moments when Mac's music filled the air were some of the most peaceful she'd known since she'd awakened nearly naked on the streets of Bitterroot after her captivity.

He began to sing and she warmed even more. He sang like an angel. His voice was deep and pure and utterly amazing. Unfortunately he only sang for a moment and then set the guitar aside.

"All we're going to do now is stand in the middle of the corral. We need to show Spirit that she's in our space and not vice versa."

They both got up from the chairs and walked to the gate in the corral. He led the way to the center of the wooden structure and then stopped. She stood beside him while Buddy watched from just outside the corral.

Spirit responded by quickly swishing her tail and dancing backward until her hindquarters hit the far railing. Her eyes widened and her nostrils flared.

"Just act naturally. She's frightened. We have to show her that we aren't going to hurt her, that we're not a threat to her in any way," Mac said. "But we also have to show that we have a right to be in here with her."

"I just want to wrap my arms around her neck and magically take all her pain and heal her from whatever trauma she's experienced," she replied.

Mac smiled. "It would be nice if a hug was really that powerful. You know I vaguely remember you from high school although you were a couple of years younger than me. Didn't you become a cheerleader?"

"Yes, I was a cheerleader from my sophomore to my senior year."

"And weren't you homecoming queen and, if I remember right, you were also Miss Bitterroot at the fall festival one year."

She eyed him warily and a slight flutter of tension filled her. "You seem to have a very good memory."

He shrugged easily. "It's a small town. It's easy to remember people and events."

"Yeah, well, that was my past and things have changed since then," she replied rather curtly. She didn't want to remember those fun, carefree years. That girl was gone forever, murdered by the man who had kidnapped her and held her for what had seemed like an eternity.

Mac looked at her for a long moment, his gaze warm as it lingered. "Marisa, I can't begin to imagine what kind of a nightmare you had to endure, but I'm so sorry it all happened to you. I'm just really glad you're safe and sound and here right now."

She straightened her back and looked for any signs of pity in the depths of his brown eyes. Thankfully, she saw none there. Instead, she thought, she saw a faint admiration. She could live with that, even though she doubted that he'd approve of what she intended to do next in her life. "Thank you," she finally said.

He looked off toward the big house in the distance. "It must be nice to be living so close to your mother."

She released a dry laugh. "Have you met my mother?"

"Only in passing," he replied.

"She isn't exactly the warm and fuzzy type. We've never been real close, but we're definitely not on the best of terms right now. According to her, I have been nothing more than a source of embarrassment for her. She believes my abduction was somehow my fault and I dragged the Lindale name through a big scandal." She clamped her mouth shut, irritated that she'd shared far more than she'd intended.

"I'm so sorry to hear that," he replied. "Victim blaming is never a good thing."

"It is what it is," she replied. She had long ago made peace with the fact that she and her mother shared different value systems and she would never, ever be able to live up to her mother's expectations of her.

She'd definitely been a daddy's girl. Her father had been her hero, supporting her in everything she did and providing a loving buffer between her and her cold, controlling mother. God, there were days when she still missed him so much.

They fell silent, and then, after a few minutes, Mac pulled a small, shiny red apple out of his pocket and held it out toward the frightened mare.

Although Spirit's eyes widened once again, she raised her head and appeared to sniff the air. "Horses are naturally inquisitive creatures," he said. "She can see and can probably smell this apple and her curiosity is piqued, but she's still too frightened to step forward and check it out."

"You think eventually she'll trust us enough to do that?" she asked. Right now the idea of the frightened horse eating anything out of his hand seemed impossible.

"We can hope so, but only time will tell," he said.

"Thank you for not giving me some fairy-tale

answer like I'm going to be on her back in a week riding off into the sunset of happily-ever-after."

Once again he held her gaze. It was as if he was attempting to look deep into her soul. "Would that be your idea of a happily-ever-after?"

"To be honest, I don't think much about happily-ever-afters anymore. Now, how about some lunch? I have the makings of ham-and-cheese sandwiches."

He blinked, as if trying to process her quick change of subject. "I really didn't expect you to feed me anything," he replied. He changed the apple from one hand to the other. "But if you're offering I wouldn't turn down a sandwich."

"I'll be right back." She needed to get away from him for a few minutes. She needed to get away and regain her equilibrium. He was far too easy to talk to and their conversation had become far too personal.

She had a feeling it would be dangerously easy for her to fall into the warm softness in his eyes, and to lose sight of her ultimate goal. She couldn't allow that to happen.

When she went back outside with their lunch she would make sure to establish better boundaries with him. No matter how drawn to him she was, she had to keep him at arm's length and remember he was just a man here to train her horse.

Chapter 3

As Mac stepped out of his room, his stomach gurgled with hunger. Several of the men had made plans to meet and eat at the café tonight instead of having dinner at the ranch. It felt like it had been a long time since he'd eaten the sandwich Marisa had served him that afternoon.

Sawyer Quincy, the ranch foreman and one of the original boys who had arrived on the ranch along with Mac, was meeting him for dinner. So were Dusty and Jerod Steen, who had recently gotten married and left the Holiday ranch.

The other person who would be at the café was Flint McCay, who had recently quit the ranch and moved into a beautiful cabin in the woods with his wife, Madison.

It had been a while since Mac had seen Flint and Jerod, so he was looking forward to catching up with the two over the evening meal.

He checked his watch and then headed to the vehicle shed. Minutes later, as he drove toward town, he couldn't help thinking of his time at Marisa's that day.

The more time he spent with her, the more intrigued he was by her. This morning's conversation had flowed pretty easily, but there had been a marked change in her mood when she'd brought out the sandwiches for lunch. After they had eaten she'd been decidedly cooler and completely closed off to any conversation that didn't pertain to the horse.

She'd asked him questions about the training of the horse and about what she should be doing when he wasn't there, but her demeanor didn't invite any further personal questions or talk.

All three times he'd seen her she had been dressed in black. Despite the gun she wore on her hip she reminded him of a sleek, shapely female ninja. She was all mystery, with her beautiful but guarded eyes and her dark persona.

He'd left her place at three and had come back to the ranch with plans made for him to return the next day, after his work finished.

She should be just another client who had hired him for his services. But he'd never had another client before who lingered in his thoughts long after he'd left them. He'd never had a client whose nearness warmed him like hers did. Even when he tried to keep thoughts of her out of his head, it didn't work.

Once again he tried to shove her out of his thoughts as he pulled down Main Street. On a Saturday night the café was always busy and Mac had to park down the block from the establishment. He immediately spied Dusty nearby, getting out of his truck. He grinned as Mac approached him.

"Tricia couldn't wait for me to get out of the house tonight," he told Mac as they fell into step together. "She was thrilled not to have to plan or cook any dinner for me."

"Well, I'm just glad you're here even though I had to look at your ugly mug for most of the day today," Mac replied.

"Ha, I'm not here to have dinner with you. I'm looking forward to seeing Jerod and Flint," Dusty retorted. "And speak of those two devils…" Jerod and Flint were heading toward the café from the opposite direction.

They all met at the front door, and greetings were exchanged. "Where's Sawyer?" Flint asked. "I thought he was meeting us, too. Is he just running late?"

"He had to take a rain check. Apparently Janis is off tonight and she had planned something special for the two of them," Dusty said. Sawyer's wife was a waitress at the popular bar, The Watering Hole.

"Oh, sounds like something good for Sawyer," Jerod said with one of his slow grins.

They all laughed and then walked into the busy café. Delicious scents mixed with the clinking of silverware and the chattering of the dozens of diners that filled the room.

Flint spied an empty booth toward the back and they all finally sat. Mac looked around the place, seeing several friends from other ranches and a table full of men from the Humes ranch.

Mac grimaced as he met the gaze of Zeke Osmond, a man who was always at the center of trouble. Zeke grinned at Mac and then turned and said something to the other three at his table. They all looked over at the Holiday men and then guffawed.

Just looking at Zeke irritated Mac. Zeke was small but wiry. His dark hair was long and always looked unwashed and greasy. He had gray eyes... beady and untrustworthy.

Mac ignored the men at the other table and opened the menu in front of him. The last thing he wanted was for them to stress him out. Within minutes their waitress had arrived to take their orders.

As they waited for the food, they caught up with each other's lives. Flint talked about his happy new life at his cabin. He was still trying to figure out what he might want to do next after quitting the Holiday ranch. Madison was pregnant and Flint couldn't wait for the baby to be born.

She'd had a rough time several months ago, when she was sexually assaulted and beaten up by the mayor's son, Brad Ainsworth. It had been a huge scandal, but thankfully, Brad was in jail and Madison and Flint had fallen in love and married.

Jerod was loving his life with his new wife, Lily, who was currently pregnant, too. He was enjoying being the father figure to Lily's nine-year-old son, Caleb.

Hearing all the talk about kids and family reminded Mac of what he had once yearned for…a family of his own and babies to sing to. He was vaguely surprised to realize that the yearning was still there. He'd thought he'd completely squashed it out of his mind and heart, but a tiny bit of it still remained.

"How are things at the ranch?" Flint asked.

"Okay, but we had a fence down the other day. Five cows disappeared and have never been found," Mac replied.

"I smell cattle thieves sitting at that table over

there." Jerod nodded his head toward the table where the men from their neighboring ranch sat.

"You got that right," Dusty said. "Things had been pretty quiet with them for the last couple of months, but you never know when their ugly will show up again."

"And their only goal is to stir up trouble for Cassie," Flint muttered with obvious disgust.

"Please, let's not talk about them anymore," Mac pleaded. "It's going to ruin my appetite."

The rest of the men agreed and by that time the waitress arrived with their food. Mac and Flint had ordered the Saturday-night special of chicken-fried steak with mashed potatoes and gravy. Dusty and Jerod had both got burgers and fries.

As they dove into their food, it didn't stop their conversation from flowing. They talked about ranching issues and the preparations for the coming of winter. They teased Flint about being cozied in at his log cabin in the woods with his wife and a roaring fire.

"If she wasn't already pregnant then I would figure by December Madison would have been pregnant anyway," Dusty said and then laughed as Flint's cheeks turned red.

"Ha, look who's talking, Mr. Daddy times two," Flint countered, and again laughter went around the table as they all teased Dusty.

"I hear you're working with a new horse," Jerod said to Mac when they'd finally sobered.

"How did you hear that?" Mac asked.

"Dusty told me," Jerod replied.

Mac released a small laugh. "I should have known." He looked at Dusty and then back at Jerod. "He's always got his nose in everybody's business."

"No, I don't," Dusty protested. "I just like to keep everyone informed on what everyone else is doing. It helps us all stay connected to each other."

Mac smiled at Dusty. Of all the cowboys who had come to the Holiday ranch when they'd been nothing more than kids, Dusty had the softest, most open heart. "I was just joking," Mac said. "Besides, we'll always be connected as brothers."

"You got that right," Flint replied.

Mac looked at Jerod. "And yes, I'm working with a new horse. She's going to be a real challenge."

"I heard she belongs to Marisa Lindale," Flint said.

"She does," Mac replied and offered no other information. It was odd, but he was somehow reluctant to share much of anything about the woman he was working for. He felt oddly protective of her. "The horse looks like she's been badly abused, so she's going to take plenty of work."

"Ah, hell, Mac, you'll use your magic music

voodoo and have that mare dancing to your tune before no time at all," Flint said.

Mac laughed. "We'll have to see about that. Only time will tell how it will go." He was grateful when none of them asked him questions about Marisa.

As they continued to eat they talked about town events and the fall festival that had just happened. The café continued to fill with more people out for the evening meal.

The din grew louder with laughter and chatter. The waitresses were kept busy running from tables to booths and back, making sure everyone in their sections was happy.

The noise suddenly stuttered to an unexpected silence. Mac turned around to see what had caused everyone to stop talking at the same time.

She stood just inside the entrance, a lone diner clad in her usual black.

Marisa.

Her chin lifted and she had a look of determination as she moved to an empty two-top table. She reminded Mac of a soldier going into battle all alone. Once she sat, the chatter in the café resumed, and there was no question the conversations going on were all about her.

"Wow, this has got to be her first time out in public," Dusty said.

"I didn't even know she was back in town until yesterday when you told me, Dusty," Flint said.

"Excuse me for just a moment." Mac slid out of his seat. He placed his napkin next to his plate and then approached Marisa's table. "Hi, Marisa," he greeted her with a friendly smile. "It's so nice to see you out and about."

"I thought it was about time for me to get out of the cabin," she replied. She offered him a small, slightly nervous-looking smile in return. "Besides, I was getting sick of my own cooking."

"I can highly recommend the Saturday-night special," he replied.

She picked up the menu in front of her. "Thanks, Mac, I'll keep that in mind."

"Well, I just wanted to stop by and say hello." What he'd really wanted to do was assure her she had a friend in here.

"And I really appreciate it, Mac."

He started to back away from the table, but he bumped into Zeke Osmond, who practically shoved Mac out of the way.

"Oh my God… Marisa. I didn't know you were back in town and just as beautiful as ever," Zeke gushed and swiped his long, greasy hair away from his eyes.

Although Mac wanted to somehow protect her from the slimy, dark-haired creep, he returned to his own seat as Marisa greeted Zeke. It certainly wasn't his job to shield her from old acquaintances in town.

He was glad she'd made a public appearance and gotten out of the isolation of the cabin. He hoped it was a first step in her reclaiming her life here in Bitterroot. He really wished she could find the kind of peace that would chase away the darkness and secrets he saw in her beautiful eyes.

It had taken everything Marisa possessed in her power to get out of her car and walk into the café. Instantly she'd felt everyone's gaze on her as a stifling silence descended. Then the talking had begun once again. She saw the furtive glances cast her way and knew she was the subject of all the conversations going on.

It was definitely disconcerting and she was surprised by how grateful she'd been when Mac had come over to greet her. Before that moment, she'd felt like some kind of a pariah.

Mac's greeting seemed to break the ice with everyone else. She'd gone to high school with Zeke Osmond and at that time everyone had known Zeke had a big crush on her. Was he the one? Had Zeke gone to Oklahoma City almost two years ago and grabbed her, blindfolded her, and then drugged her and kept her someplace dark and dank for sixty agonizing days?

Or had it been Brendon Timber, another high

school friend who'd stopped by her table to say hello? She knew from her mother that Brendon worked as a ranch hand on the Lindale ranch, but Marisa had never seen him around on the property or her cabin.

Whoever her attacker was, she hoped he saw her out. She desperately wanted him to see that she was doing just fine and living her best life. Even though she had been kidnapped in Oklahoma City, he'd let her know he was from her hometown. Just before he had released her, he'd promised he'd come for her again and the next time he'd never let her go.

She wanted him to come for her again. She was praying he would try to take her once again. This time she was more than ready for him and he would pay for those sixty long days of torture she had endured at his hands.

She hoped he was in the café right now, but if he wasn't, he would eventually see her. She intended to give up her self-imposed isolation now and be seen around on the streets of Bitterroot.

When the waitress arrived at her table she ordered a chef's salad and a decaf coffee. Even though she appreciated Mac vouching for the Saturday-night special, there was no way she was going to load up on a bunch of carbs that might only make her sluggish after eating.

She considered herself to still be in training to

deal with a psychopath. As she ate her meal, several more people paused by her table to say hello and tell her how great it was that she was back in her hometown. It was obvious that nobody had realized she'd been back in Bitterroot for almost a year now.

They would all know she was back in town now and she didn't care how her presence here might upset her mother or the sensibilities of her mother's cronies. If Rose Lindale had her way Marisa would either move out of state or stay locked away unseen and unheard in the cabin forever, especially now with her own plans to run for mayor.

Marisa finished her meal, but lingered over coffee. People left the café and more people entered. Some of them spoke to her with warmth and friendliness while others simply stared at her unabashedly.

By seven thirty she was aware of night shadows beginning to move in and suddenly she was eager to leave and get back inside the safety of her cabin. She was sorry that Buddy wasn't waiting for her in her car and that she had chosen to leave him at home for the evening.

She paid her bill and then walked out of the café. As she hurried to her car she kept her purse open in case she would have to reach in and pull out the gun that nestled inside. She also had a wicked-sharp knife tucked down into the top of her knee-high leather boots. Anytime she was out of the cabin she was armed.

She breathed a sigh of relief once she was in the safe confines of her vehicle. However, she didn't fully relax. As she drove back home she kept her gaze divided between the road ahead and the rear-view mirror. She needed to see if anyone was following her.

In the very depths of her gut, she didn't believe he would come after her tonight, or anytime in the next week or two. If he stayed true to the ritual… to the way it had all happened last time, the torture would begin with him making phone calls to her and mailing her threatening letters.

When the calls and letters had started in Oklahoma City, she'd believed they were just stupid pranks. The caller's voice had been mechanical, obviously masked by some sort of voice app, and the calls were always anonymous, with no phone number displayed on her caller ID. The letters were placed in her mailbox with no postage stamp.

"I've always seen you, but you don't see me."

"You will be mine," the letters and the distorted voice had said.

She'd assumed that whoever it was, they had the wrong number, the wrong person. Still, for two weeks she'd received the strange calls and notes, and then they had stopped. And a week later she'd been taken…dragged out of her car by a man wearing a ski mask.

But even if he didn't make the chilling calls or leave her threatening notes before attempting to kidnap her this time, she was ready for him. She had spent the last eighteen months preparing for him.

Once she reached the Lindale ranch, she drove toward the barn where she parked her vehicle. Darkness had almost taken over the landscape as she got out of the car. She pulled her gun from her purse and a flashlight from the car and then began to walk to the cabin in the distance.

A cool night breeze had picked up, stirring fall leaves on the trees that crackled and crunched as they brushed against each other. She kept on guard, listening for any sound that didn't belong to nature.

She didn't relax until she stepped into the cabin and Buddy greeted her with a happy bark. She gave him some loving and then let him outside to do his business before bedtime.

By the time she let him back inside she'd already put on her night clothes. She was satisfied with her night's work. Tomorrow she intended to take a leisurely walk down Main Street and then Mac would be here in the evening.

She was surprised by the fact that thoughts of the handsome man warmed her in places she hadn't been warm for a very long time. She'd appreciated him stopping by her table to tell her hello. It had felt like she'd found a friend in an alien and hostile environment. It also seemed to have encouraged many of the other diners in the café to be friendly to her.

She got into bed and drifted off to sleep, and immediately fell into nightmares of being poked and prodded in the dark, of a disembodied voice's maniacal laughter. The darkness held danger, and for sixty long and agonizing days there had been no light. There were times when she'd felt the pinprick of a needle in the darkness and knew she would fall unconscious from whatever drug he'd injected her with.

At one point she'd awakened to find herself bound and blindfolded and on some kind of a table. Then the tattooing had begun. Now, in her dreams, the pain on her right hip screamed through her as pinpricks dug deep into her flesh.

She jerked awake to Buddy whining and licking the side of her face. Tears chased down her cheeks and she buried her head in Buddy's soft fur and drew in deep, steadying breaths.

It was only in her nightmares that she cried. When she was awake she never allowed herself the weakness of tears. She had cried for sixty long days and nights, and that had been more than enough for a lifetime.

She gave Buddy a final hug, swiped at her cheeks and then sat up. A glance at the clock on her nightstand let her know that it was after six and dawn had arrived.

As she went about her morning routine she thought about the night before. She considered her trip to the café a big success. By now the gossip that she was out and about in town would have made the rounds. Hopefully, if *he* hadn't been in the café he still had probably heard the news.

By noon she was ready to leave her cabin once again for a walk down Main Street. Even though it was Sunday, all the stores would be open by now and people would be out.

She dressed in a pair of black jeans and pulled on a bright red lightweight sweater. She didn't want to wear black today. She definitely wanted to stand out and be seen.

It was another beautiful early fall day. Thankfully, the temperatures had climbed to slightly above normal for this time of the year. She parked in the center of Main Street and then got out of the car.

There were plenty of other people out enjoying the mild weather. As she walked down the sidewalk she noticed some new stores that hadn't been there the last time she'd visited that part of town.

When she'd first moved to Oklahoma City, she'd thought to make it her permanent home.

She'd enjoyed the absence of her mother's constant judgment and watchful eye, and believed the distance from home would help her to grow and flourish.

And for a while she had. She'd had a job she loved and a cute little apartment that felt like home. She'd dated often, but the man of her dreams had remained elusive. Still, she'd been happy...until her life had been brutally stolen from her.

Now, as she leisurely walked, she realized there was a part of her that had missed her hometown. She had missed the small-town feel that permeated Bitterroot. Despite her father's death and her strained relationship with her mother, she'd spent many happy years here.

As she continued down the sidewalk, some of the people she met greeted her with friendly smiles and others walked by and averted their gaze from her. She understood that some people wouldn't know what to say to her and that was okay.

All that was really important to her was that the man who had kidnapped her knew she was living her life without fear, that she was back home and was doing just fine. She wanted to bait him into coming after her again. A reunion with the creep was what she most wanted in her life.

"Marisa." Zeke Osmond approached her from

the opposite direction with a big smile on his face. "Hey, how are you doing?"

"I'm doing fine. How about you?" She couldn't help wondering if he was the man who had destroyed her life.

"I'm doing just great," he replied. "We didn't get much of a chance to really visit last night in the café. I was wondering if maybe you'd be up for me taking you to The Watering Hole one night for some two-stepping fun." His small eyes quickly eyed her from head to toe, immediately making her feel like she needed to take a hot shower.

"Zeke, I'm sorry, but I'm still settling in and I'm not really open to dating right now."

"Are you staying with your mother?" he asked.

Her muscles tensed. "No, not in the big house. I'm staying at the foreman's cabin on the back of the property." Had she just given her attacker her home address? Had Zeke been the man who had kidnapped and held her and was he now ready to do it all over again? Right now almost every man in Bitterroot was a potential suspect.

"Why don't I give you my phone number so if you change your mind about going out some night, you can give me a call?" Zeke replied.

Marisa withdrew her phone from her purse and handed it to Zeke. He placed his number in her contacts list and then put her number into his. They said their goodbyes to each other and moved on.

If the phone calls began, then she'd have to seriously consider Zeke a suspect. Only a few people had her phone number, and most who did were clients.

She wound up in a shoe store and bought herself a pair of nice gray knee-high boots. After making the purchase she walked a little farther and then went into the café to eat lunch.

The meal went much as her dinner had the night before. A lot of people who hadn't seen her last night greeted her with surprised, yet friendly smiles. Others, especially a few of her mother's friends, pointedly ignored her. That was fine with her. She didn't need their approval to survive.

When she left the café she almost bumped into two women walking in. "Marisa? Marisa Lindale…oh my goodness…is that really you?"

Marisa immediately recognized the two, even though it had been almost ten years since she'd last seen them. "Yes, it's really me. Hi, Sissy… Kim."

Sissy Atwater and Kim Cordell had been cheerleaders and best friends with Marisa all through high school. Sissy clapped her hands together, her blue eyes merry as she grinned at Marisa.

"So you're back in town to stay?" Sissy didn't wait for her answer. "Oh my goodness, this is so exciting. We totally have to get together and catch up. After you left town I married Ryan Beal and Kim married Chuck Phelps."

"And I have a four-year-old little girl and Sissy has five-year-old twin boys. Can you believe it?" Kim said and then laughed. "And I still remember the time the three of us vowed that we would never let a boy put his tongue in our mouths when we got a kiss."

"Times have definitely changed," Sissy said.

They all laughed and exchanged phone numbers. "I can't believe you cut off your gorgeous hair," Kim said.

"I just got tired of dealing with it," Marisa replied. The truth of the matter was she'd cut it short after going through some of the self-protection classes. Long hair was easy for an attacker to grab and use to inflict pain and subdue a person.

"I think the short cut suits you," Sissy said. "It really highlights your beautiful eyes."

"Thanks, Sis," Marisa replied.

They chitchatted for a few more minutes, and then the two women went on into the café and Marisa headed to her car. The women remained in her thoughts as she drove home.

The three of them had been thick as thieves all through school. They had spent time at each other's homes and had shared secrets and dreams of the future. Many of their fantasies had revolved around getting married and having children. It sounded like the two of them had achieved that.

At one time that was what Marisa had wished for, too.

Instantly a vision of Mac filled her mind. He was definitely the kind of man she had once dreamed about for her future. Handsome and kind, respectful and sexy. She only wished she had met him before she'd left Bitterroot, before her dreams had all been shattered.

But surely she was only thinking about him right now because he would be arriving at the cabin soon to work with Spirit?

Yesterday he had added his voice to the guitar and his deep, smooth, absolutely beautiful singing voice had brought on the warmth of a whiskey shot sliding down her throat and bursting heat into her stomach. She could have listened to him for hours.

She found herself interested in him, in his past and in his everyday life. Still, it was odd that when she remembered those old dreams of love and family, thoughts of him should suddenly fill her mind.

Not that it mattered. She didn't dream about love and marriage and having a family anymore.

All she dreamed about was torture and death.

She was back. He'd known she would eventually show up here again, and every nerve in his body screamed with excitement. Despite the fact that she'd cut her long hair off since the last time he'd seen her, she was still the most beautiful woman in the entire world.

He wanted her. Oh, he didn't want to possess her physically. He really didn't even want to touch her. He'd loved her at one time, but now he hated her with a vengeance he'd never felt before.

He now wanted her as badly as he had the first time when he'd taken her from her parking lot in Oklahoma City. Oh, it had been magical, it had been absolutely amazing to possess her and humiliate and control her.

Those sixty days had been the best he'd ever had in his entire life. He'd thought about keeping her forever…of punishing her forever, but as he'd remembered the rush of capturing her, he wanted it all over again, and that was why he'd ultimately decided to let her go.

Taking her again was exactly what he intended to do. He'd give her some time to feel safe again, and then the games would begin. She was like an elusive butterfly to him. He'd toy with her and then he'd capture her.

And this time he would never, ever let her go.

Chapter 4

Mac got out of his truck and grabbed his guitar case. Once again he was at Marisa's to work with her horse. This time he was surprised to see the folding chairs already set up and Marisa seated in one, with Buddy at her feet.

"Good evening," he said in greeting. As usual, she looked beautiful in a black pair of leggings that hugged her slender, shapely legs and a black-and-gray-striped long sweater. Knee-high gray boots hugged the length of her legs. "Have you been out here awhile, waiting for me?"

"Not long, but I decided to come out a little early and enjoy this beautiful weather."

"It is a gorgeous evening," he agreed.

For the first time since he'd begun coming to her cabin, Buddy didn't growl as Mac sank down in the chair next to hers. "We are definitely on borrowed time with this nice weather. Winter is really just right around the corner."

"Even knowing that, I still love autumn," she replied.

"Me, too," he said with a smile. "Does she ever go into the stall in the shed?" he asked and gestured to the horse.

"I've never seen her go inside, but we haven't had any rain or bad weather since she was delivered here to me. Hopefully, when we do, she'll want to use the stall in the shed."

Mac smiled at Marisa. "I hear through the grapevine you've been out and about again today."

"It's nice to know the Bitterroot grapevine is still alive and well," she replied wryly. "I actually went into town to buy me a new pair of boots." She lifted her feet to show him the knee-high boots.

"Nice," he said. The boots were not only nice, but he found them very sexy on her. She never sat out here with him without a gun and holster around her waist and tonight was no exception.

She was a woman painted in contrasts. She appeared hard and edgy, but her eyes sometimes reflected a hint of soft vulnerability. She rarely smiled, but when she did, there was more than a touch of warmth that seemed to struggle to get free.

Each evening he spent with her, despite the coming of darkness, he didn't want to leave. He wanted more time with her. Every minute he spent with her only made him want to know her better.

He'd like to take her out to dinner someplace where they could sit across from each other over a candle-lit meal. He'd love to ride a pasture with her and see her head thrown back in laughter. He had to keep reminding himself he was here about the horse and not the woman. However, it was difficult when the woman was so appealing to him.

"Are you ready for a little music?" he asked as he took his guitar out of its case.

She gave him one of her rare smiles. "I'm always ready to hear a little of your music. Are you going to sing again tonight?"

He returned her smile. Yesterday had been the first time he'd put his voice with his guitar. "Maybe, if you sing along with me."

"Oh no, I can't sing anything like you can," she protested.

"That doesn't matter. As far as I'm concerned, everyone should sing something every day. It's good for the soul. Besides, you should hear the caterwauling of some of the cowboys at the ranch when I play the guitar for them."

She laughed. It was the first time he'd heard her

laughter. It was a deep and rich, throaty sound that rolled through him and he hugged the sound to his heart. He instantly wanted to hear it again… and again.

"When Sawyer Quincy used to sing with us at night, he sounded like a cross between a disgruntled rooster and a buzz saw," he continued. "And my friend Dusty couldn't find a tune if one jumped into his hat and he plopped it on his head, but that doesn't stop him from singing loud and strong."

"Stop," she said. "You're making me laugh."

He eyed her curiously. "Is that such a bad thing?"

She broke eye contact with him and looked away in the distance. "It's just been a very long time since I've had anything to laugh about."

"Maybe while I'm here working with Spirit we can change that." He hesitated a moment and she once again met his gaze. "Just so you know, Marisa, I'm definitely not part of the Bitterroot grapevine crowd. You never have to worry about anything that happens here or the conversations between you and me going any further."

She held his gaze for several long seconds, and then nodded. "Thank you, Mac. I appreciate that."

He began to strum his guitar and looked over at Spirit, who cocked her head and twitched her ears in response. "Notice that she didn't back up tonight," he remarked.

"I noticed that. Maybe it means this all will take less time than we initially thought."

"Maybe or maybe not," he said and continued to strum. "It's always hard to predict animal behavior. Have you been coming out during the day to talk to her?"

"Every afternoon," she said. "I walk around the corral and talk to her, but she never takes her eyes off me and she never lets me get anywhere close to her. Now, why don't you sing something for me…uh…sing something for her?"

She immediately covered her slip of the tongue by shifting positions in her chair and looking toward Spirit. Mac sang two country-Western ballads and then set the guitar down, vaguely disappointed that she didn't sing along. He finished the second one and looked at her. "Let's head into the corral."

"Did you bring your magic apple?"

He laughed. "Always." He pulled the small red apple from his pocket. "But I'm beginning to think it's not so magical after all."

"Oh, I don't know. Sometimes when I see you standing in the middle of the corral holding it out, it reminds me of something and I want to tell Spirit, who is really a princess in disguise, not to trust any shiny, polished apples."

He laughed, delighted that she not only had a real sense of humor, but was feeling comfortable enough to show it to him. "I can promise you and Spirit that it's not a poisoned apple."

"I'll give her the memo."

They walked into the corral and Mac took up his usual stance in the center of the enclosure with the apple in his hand. Marisa stood next to him, and as usual he was acutely aware of her nearness to him.

Her wild, evocative scent seemed to call to something wild and free inside him. And the energy that wafted from her felt warmer and softer this evening.

As he took a step closer to the mare, Spirit didn't move back but rather remained in place, although her tail swished back and forth with agitation and her nostrils flared.

"When a horse swishes their tail like she's doing right now, you always need to proceed cautiously. Sometimes tail swishing is followed by kicking," he explained.

"So she's angry, but surely that's better than her being so terrified."

"Not necessarily. It's been my experience, both with humans and horses, that often anger is just a mask for fear."

She looked at him curiously. "How did you wind up being one of Cass Holiday's lost boys?"

she asked and then instantly looked at him apologetically. "I'm sorry, first for overstepping any personal boundaries, and second, for using the term 'lost boys.'"

"Don't apologize on either count," he said hurriedly, hoping to put her at ease. "We referred to ourselves as the lost boys. However, back then there were a lot of people in town who referred to us in much worse terms."

Oh, how he remembered the things some of them had said about the twelve young boys who had come to the Holiday ranch for a second chance at life. People said they'd steal Cass blind, that they were all lowlifes and street thugs and Cass would be sorry for bringing them to her ranch. All the negativity had only bonded the twelve boys closer together.

"The last thing I would want is to offend you in any way," Marisa replied.

He smiled. "No offense taken." He changed the apple from one hand to the other as he thought about the life events that had brought him to the Holiday ranch.

"I already told you that my mother passed away when I was twelve. My father had always been a drinker, but after her death it got pretty bad and he could sometimes be a pretty mean drunk."

He paused, surprised by the wealth of negative emotions that welled up inside him as he went back to that time. However, maybe if he shared with her what had happened to him, then she would be more open to sharing some things with him.

"Anyway, when my mother would take me for guitar lessons, I always used one of my instructor's guitars because I didn't have one of my own. After my mom's death the lessons stopped and all I wanted was a guitar of my own." He'd desperately wanted a guitar of his own to honor his mother by continuing to play the music she'd so loved.

"Your father wouldn't buy you one?" Marisa asked.

"I was afraid to even ask him. He'd always said the music was just foolish nonsense. He even sold the piano soon after my mother's death. I knew he wouldn't buy me one. The kind of guitar I wanted wasn't cheap, so I started doing odd jobs and mowing lawns around the neighborhood. I did whatever I could to make money that I secretly tucked away. Finally, when I'd just turned fourteen, I had enough to buy the guitar of my dreams."

"That must have been an exciting day for you," Marisa said softly.

"Oh, it was. I was so proud and so happy. I ran to the music store and bought the guitar and then I ran home and went to my bedroom and began to play. I played some of the songs my mother had loved to hear. I know it sounds crazy, but it felt like a connection with my mother."

"That doesn't sound crazy at all," she said.

He smiled at her gratefully, but his smile slid from his face as he thought about what had happened next. "I was sitting on my bed playing one of my mom's favorite songs when my door suddenly burst open. I could immediately tell that my father was stinking drunk and in a dangerous mood."

Mac's hand tightened on the apple as he continued. "He started screaming about it being a waste of money, and then he grabbed the guitar out of my hands and began to beat me with it. He beat me with the guitar until it was nothing more than splintered wood."

Mac's stomach clenched as the memory of not only the emotional pain but also the physical pain rushed through him. "When he finally left my room, I packed a bag, took what little money I had and went out the window. I wasn't going to live in a world without music and I definitely wasn't going to live with a man who thought it was okay to beat me."

"And then what happened? Where did you go?"

"I lived on the streets of Oklahoma City for about four months. I got a job sweeping up the floors after hours in a beauty shop and the owner paid me in cash. She paid me just enough to get food for the day. I slept under a bridge and fought to protect what little I had."

"It must have been rough," she said softly.

"It was. It was a scary time in my life," he admitted. "I wanted something better for myself, but I was too young to see a way out. When a social worker approached me about working on a ranch and promised that if I worked hard there would be a roof over my head and three meals a day, I jumped at the chance. She took me to Big Cass Holiday's ranch and that's my story."

To his surprise, she reached out and took his hand in hers. Her eyes radiated a warm compassion. "I'm so sorry you had to go through that. I can't imagine a young boy who was afraid to go home and basically cast out onto the streets." She immediately released his hand.

It was the first time she'd willingly touched him and the feel of her warm, smaller hand in his lingered long after she removed it.

"Thanks, Marisa. But what I went through in my past can't begin to compare to what you endured at the hands of a madman. I hope in time you'll trust me enough to talk about it with me."

Their gazes remained locked and in the depths of her eyes, which were now more gray than blue, he saw the haunting and a whisper of vulnerability. It was there only a moment and then gone.

She crossed her arms defensively and her eyes went blank. "We'll see," she finally said. "Isn't it time we take a walk around the corral before it gets too late?"

"Absolutely," he agreed. He tucked the small apple into his jacket pocket and then the two of them left the corral and took a slow walk around the wooden enclosure.

Their conversation remained impersonal, focusing on the weather and the next holiday, which was Halloween. "I don't think you need to prepare for too many trick-or-treaters out here," he said.

"I'm sure I won't get any, but that won't stop me from buying a big bag of candy and then eating it all myself."

"Ah, so you have a sweet tooth," he replied in a teasing tone.

"Definitely, especially when it comes to anything chocolate." She looked at him curiously. "What about you? Are you a sweets kind of guy?"

"I'm not much into candy or cakes, but I do love pie, especially apple pie. However, if apple isn't available, I'll eat almost any kind there is," he replied.

"I used to make pies, but I haven't in a long time. It seems kind of silly to make one for just one person," she said.

He imagined there were a lot of things she didn't do anymore. He was pleased to see that as they continued around the corral, Spirit watched them but didn't move in response to them. The horse appeared a little less threatened by them tonight.

"Did you enjoy living in Oklahoma City?" he asked, hoping he wasn't overstepping boundaries.

"I did," she replied easily. "I had a job I enjoyed and a nice apartment and a group of good friends I loved hanging out with."

"Are you planning to eventually go back there?"

"I'm not sure…but I don't think so. It feels good to be back home in Bitterroot. I know right now I'm something of a freak show, but once people get used to seeing me around that will fade."

"You are definitely not a freak show," he protested adamantly.

She flashed him her elusive, beautiful smile. "Thanks, Mac."

By the time they'd made it around the corral two times, the shadows of night were closing in and he could feel her tension growing. They folded up the chairs and carried them to the shed.

"I'll walk you to your door," he said, sensing her nervousness with the coming of darkness.

He fell into step with her and Buddy and the three of them walked toward the cabin door. "Same time tomorrow?" he asked.

"That's the plan, but I have an appointment

for service at four at Wright's Car Dealership," she said.

"Are you having car trouble?"

She nodded. "I'm pretty sure I just need a new battery, so it shouldn't take too long." They reached the door and she opened it to allow Buddy to go on inside, then turned back to him.

"Don't let Larry try to talk you into any expensive repairs that you don't need. He can be kind of a bully."

She offered him one of her rare smiles. "Don't worry. I don't bully easily." She took a step toward him, suddenly standing intimately close. "Thank you for sharing your past with me." Her voice was a whisper of warm breath on his face.

"No problem." He wanted to kiss her. God, he wanted to taste her lips. All he had to do was lean forward a little bit more. Her lips parted as if in anticipation. However, before he could act, she stepped back and the moment was lost.

"Good night, Mac," she said.

"Good night, Marisa. I'll see you tomorrow."

He remained on her stoop until her door closed and he heard the click of a lock. He shoved his hands into his jeans pocket and turned around and walked to his truck.

Once he was headed back to the ranch, he tried to focus on the small progress he thought they were making with Spirit, but it was Spirit's owner that he couldn't get out of his mind.

What might have happened if he'd taken the opportunity and kissed her? Would she have been appalled by his action or would she have welcomed it? There had been a moment when she'd looked as if she'd wanted him to kiss her, but he would never do so without asking her first.

The last thing he wanted was for him to do something...anything to alienate her or ruin the fragile relationship it felt like they were building.

Rolling down his window to let in the night air, he continued to think of her. He felt a thawing in her. He believed she was starting to trust him not just as a horse trainer but as a man. There was no question that he was intensely physically drawn to her, but it was so much more than that.

He wanted inside her head. He wanted her to share with him what she'd gone through when she was kidnapped, and tell him what he could do to help her move past the ordeal she'd suffered.

He wanted to help her to find more of her laughter, to see those beautiful eyes of hers filled with mirth instead of so many dark shadows. He wanted her smile to be a common occurrence rather than rare.

Despite her being something of a mystery and the brief time he'd known her, there was no question that he was definitely starting to fall for her.

Rather than fill him with joy, the thought set off alarm bells in his mind: if things continued the way they were going, he was probably headed for heartbreak.

After all, why would a woman as beautiful and as bright as Marisa be romantically interested in a singing cowboy who knew how to tame a horse but knew nothing about women?

The next afternoon, as Marisa drove into town for her appointment at Wright's Car Dealership, she once again thought of that moment with Mac at her front door the night before.

"That moment" had played through her head all morning. She'd thought he was going to kiss her. As they'd stood so close to each other at her door, she'd been shocked to realize that if he'd tried to kiss her, she would have let him. In fact, she had wanted him to.

She'd seen his desire for her in his eyes, but unfortunately he hadn't tried to kiss her and the moment had passed. She could admit that she was strongly attracted to him physically. And she was surprised to realize that that part of her was still alive. She'd thought it had died in the dark of sixty days in captivity.

She wouldn't be averse to exploring a physical relationship with Mac as long as he knew and understood her rules. And her first rule would be that it was strictly physical and would never become a real relationship. She couldn't afford to have it any other way.

She might be willing to share her body with him, but there was no way she planned to share anything else. The last thing she wanted was for anyone to know what was in her mind and what she intended to do in the very near future.

Shoving these thoughts aside, she turned into Wright's Car Dealership. Larry Wright owned both the only car lot and the only garage in Bitterroot. As she pulled up and parked, Larry exited the building and approached her.

Larry was a large, barrel-chested man who had a reputation for getting in people's faces. "Marisa Lindale, good to see you," he said once she was out of her car. "So, how are you adjusting to being back in Bitterroot?"

"This is my hometown. There hasn't been much need for adjusting," she replied.

"You were definitely this little town's claim to fame there for a while," Larry said. "A couple of years ago everyone was talking about you. You were the buzz of the town, a real star in the news."

What a jerk, Marisa thought. To say something like that to a woman who had survived kidnapping and captivity. "I'm here about a new battery," she said stiffly.

Larry turned toward the garage bay door. "Joe," he bellowed. "Hey, Joe. Come on out here."

A tall, lanky guy exited the bay, wiping his hands on a greasy-looking rag. He seemed vaguely familiar to her. He had light brown hair and blue eyes and he was tall and wiry-looking. "This is Marisa and she says she needs a new battery." He banged the man on the back a couple of times, causing the young man to wince slightly. "This here is Joe. He'll take good care of you." With that, Larry turned and headed back into the dealership building.

"Joe... Joe Mills?" His name suddenly popped into her head.

He gave her a shy smile. "Hi, Marisa. Uh... Larry said something about you needing a new battery. If you give me your keys I'll pull your car into the bay and take care of that for you."

She handed him the keys. "This shouldn't take too long," he said. "There's a waiting room inside if you want to wait in there."

"Thanks, Joe. I think I'll do that."

"It's just inside and to your left."

Minutes later Marisa sat in the waiting room. She was the only person there. Joe Mills...she had once wondered what had happened to him. He'd gone to high school with her, but in their junior year he had dropped out.

He'd been a shy young man who had always

sat in the back of the classrooms and often ate alone at lunchtime. One day he'd been there and the next day he was gone.

There were several people from her high school days that she remembered, and she wondered what had happened to them, if their lives had turned out happy or not. Certainly hers hadn't turned out the way she had once envisioned.

She'd spent the morning doing something she hadn't done for a very long time. She'd made an apple pie. She intended to present it to Mac this evening.

Her desire to do something nice for him had surprised her. It was a long time since she'd thought about anyone or anything other than her quest for her own personal brand of justice.

It had been surprisingly peaceful and pleasing to roll out the dough and then fill it with the fresh apple mixture. It had been satisfying to think about offering it to Mac later that evening.

True to his word, Joe finished his work quickly and twenty minutes later she was on the road and heading back home. Already she anticipated Mac coming to work with Spirit.

It wasn't just his music that reached inside her and soothed something wild; it was being around the man himself. He seemed to have such a gentle and kind soul.

At five thirty she and Buddy were already

seated in the lawn chairs when Mac pulled up and parked. His smile warmed her from head to toe as he got out and greeted her.

"Did everything go okay at the garage?" he asked once he'd settled in the chair.

"New battery in and everything went smoothly," she replied.

"And Larry didn't give you any hassles?"

"No, but he's a jerk." She related to him what Larry had said to her.

Mac's features darkened. "He's always been an insensitive bastard and what he said to you was completely out of line. I hope you didn't take any of what he said to heart."

"I didn't. There are some people you just have to ignore, and thank goodness I don't have to deal with him unless a car issue comes up," she replied. Still, she had to admit there was a little piece of her that enjoyed Mac's protective streak.

"Next time you have to go see Larry, I'd be glad to ride along. Let's see how he speaks to you then."

"Thanks, Mac. I'll keep your offer in mind."

He pulled his guitar out of the case and looked at the mare in the corral. "She seems a bit calmer again tonight," he observed.

"She does," Marisa replied.

"Maybe after a little music, we'll push her a bit by trying to get closer to her," he said.

"That sounds good." And as usual Mac smelled so good. It was a clean, woodsy fragrance that had come to represent a feeling of warmth and safety to her.

He began to strum his guitar and she relaxed into her chair. Spirit's ears perked up and forward, and to Marisa's surprise she took a couple of hesitant steps closer to the side of the corral where they sat.

"She's enjoying the music," she said.

"She definitely seems more responsive tonight in a positive manner," he replied. "She doesn't appear to think our presence out here is as much of a threat as she has in the past."

Funny, Marisa wasn't seeing Mac as being as much of a threat as she had initially. In fact, she had become quite comfortable in his company. Comfortable but with an edge of excitement and more than a whisper of desire directed toward him.

And tonight was no different. As he continued to play and began to sing softly, she found herself leaning toward him. He had the voice of an angel and if she closed her eyes and just listened, she was transported to a place of utter peace and contentment.

"Ready to do some walking?"

Her eyes snapped back open as he stopped playing and spoke. "Sure." She got up from her chair and they began their stroll around the corral.

"I think we're supposed to get some rain tomorrow," he said.

"Oh, I hate gloomy rainy days."

"Yeah, and tomorrow is my day off. I really hate it when it rains on my day off. And that means it's possible I won't be able to do much with Spirit's training."

"Maybe the weathermen will be wrong and we'll wake up to sunshine and blue skies," she said.

He laughed. "If they are wrong, it wouldn't be the first time. Sometimes I think that's the only job in the world where you can be right only half the time and still keep your job."

"True," she agreed with a bit of her own laughter. It was all so easy with him. Their conversations flowed effortlessly and their sense of humor seemed to match.

Tonight, instead of backing up in the corral to keep as far from the humans as possible, Spirit followed them as they walked around. She still kept a healthy distance, but she was definitely showing signs of being more curious…more engaged than frightened.

Once again Marisa found herself intrigued by Mac. "When did you know you had a gift with horses?" she asked.

"Almost from the beginning of my life as one of Cass's ranch hands. Many nights after my workday was over, I'd head to the stables to spend time with the horses. I had been a city boy, and I was fascinated with the creatures. Cass realized I had an interest in working with them and that I seemed to have a special bond with the animals, and she encouraged me in that."

"So, how did you learn everything you know?"

"Mostly trial and error." A deep rumble of laughter left him. She loved the sound. "I've been nipped, bit and kicked by more horses than I can remember. But I started slowly learning their language and understanding their needs and respecting them. Initially one of the other lost boys trained the horses. His name is Forest Stevens. He taught me a lot, but a couple of years ago he moved to Oklahoma City, and Cassie appointed me to train all the horses that came onto the Holiday ranch. I also started training other horses in the area for other owners."

"I heard that Cassie's aunt, Cass, was a special kind of lady."

"Oh, she was." His eyes glittered and an affectionate smile curved his lips. "She could be tough as nails with us, but she also found the best in each one of us and nurtured it. She could be the loving mother many of us hadn't had, or the tough father ready to crack the whip to keep us in line. We all grew to love her very much and none of us ever wanted to disappoint her."

"It had to be daunting for her to take in twelve young men from the streets to work her ranch," Marisa said.

"I'm sure it was, but she really had no other choice. When her husband died, all the ranch hands left because they didn't believe she was strong enough or smart enough to keep the ranch going. But she proved everyone wrong and so did we. The Holiday ranch is one of the most successful in the state now."

As he spoke, he kept his gaze trained on Spirit. Marisa could have listened to him all night long. His deep voice was like a calming drug to her.

"You must have missed her after she died in that terrible storm."

"We all grieved long and hard for her and then we wondered what would become of the ranch and us, with her gone." He motioned for her to follow him into the corral.

Once there, he pulled an apple from his jacket pocket and held it out. Spirit lifted her head and sniffed the air.

"When Cass's niece Cassie showed up, we were all certain the ranch was doomed. She and her best friend, Nicolette, had city slickers and high maintenance stamped all over them." He released another burst of his deep, sexy laughter.

"They showed up in dainty high heels and with bags of designers clothes, but it wasn't long before we realized Cassie was cut from the same cloth as Cass. She was strong and smart and soon all of us became fiercely devoted to her."

"But wasn't there a big scandal about one of the boys? And some bodies were found?" she asked.

He frowned. "Adam Benson. He was one of us but none of us knew the darkness and the demons he apparently had inside him. It wasn't until he tried to kill Cassie and he was taken out by Dillon that we learned he had been a serial killer and had buried bodies of other young men beneath a shed on the Holiday property. It was horrifying to discover somebody like that was in our midst. Not only did we feel an enormous betrayal, but we were also angry for the lives he'd stolen."

"It's frightening to know there are people who walk around with bright smiles on their faces and a horrifying evil in their hearts," she said with a deep sigh.

"Fortunately, those people are rare. I'm sorry one of those people found their way into your life."

"Thanks," she replied simply.

They fell silent for a few minutes and he took a couple of steps forward, closing the gap between him and Spirit. Tonight the horse didn't back away from him.

"Hey, pretty girl," he said softly. "Spirit, you are such a beautiful girl."

As he continued to sweet-talk the horse, a growing desire built up in Marisa. She wondered whether he would whisper sweet things in her ear if they made love? The thought was appealing.

She felt acutely aware of him tonight, more than ever before. Maybe it was because he had shared so many pieces of himself with her.

He took another step forward and finally Spirit took a step backward. He dropped his hand with the apple and shoved it back in his pocket. "I think it's just a matter of a couple more days and she'll take the apple right out of my hand," he said.

"She certainly let us much closer to her tonight." Together they left the corral.

"If it isn't raining in the morning, I'll plan on being here around ten, if that works for you. If it is raining, then I won't be by." He placed his guitar case back in his truck and then together they carried the chairs to the shed.

Her heart began to thunder with wild anticipation. She knew if she opened the cabin door to allow him entry into her home, it was actually an entry into a more personal relationship with him. There was no certainty of how things might go. The last thing she wanted was to ruin the relationship they had right now, but there was definitely a part of her that wanted more.

"Mac…before you leave, I…uh… I have a little surprise for you."

One of his dark eyebrows quirked upward. "A surprise?"

She nodded. "Do you mind coming inside for a few minutes?"

His features registered obvious puzzlement. "Sure, I can come in."

She was inviting him in for apple pie. She just didn't know at the moment if she was inviting him in for anything more.

Chapter 5

Mac had been rather shocked when Marisa told him she had a surprise for him. He was even more shocked when she invited him inside her home.

Once again he was struck by how much light there was inside the cabin as she gestured him through the door. And once again he wondered what had been done to her to make her so afraid of the dark.

However, it was her tale to tell, and right now she obviously wasn't willing to share it with him. It was very possible she might never trust enough to choose to share it with him.

"Please, have a seat." She pointed to the small

table. While he sat, she opened the oven door and pulled out a beautiful apple pie.

Buddy sank down in a doggy bed next to the sofa. Even though he appeared relaxed, his gaze shot between Mac and Marisa. He was obviously ready to spring up at the first sign of trouble to his owner.

"Oh my Lord, can you hear my stomach rumbling right now?" he asked.

She turned and gave him a full smile that momentarily stole his breath away with its beauty. "I'll admit it looks good. Let's just hope it tastes as good as it looks. It's been a long time since I baked a pie."

"What a great surprise. I can't believe you did this for me," he marveled. He was so touched that she'd not only really heard him when he mentioned that he loved apple pie, but she'd actually gone to all the trouble to make one for him. It was the nicest thing anyone had done for him in a very long time.

"I just wanted to show you my appreciation for everything you're doing here for Spirit and the friendship you've shown to me." She cut a liberal-sized piece and placed it on a small plate.

"How about a scoop of vanilla ice cream on top?"

"Oh, woman, now you're really talking my language," he replied.

She laughed, sounding more carefree than he'd ever heard her. This evening she was stunning in her black leggings and a long royal blue sweater that did amazing things to her eyes. With the smile riding her lips she looked positively enchanting.

He watched her as she scooped the ice cream and then cut another piece of the pie and put it on another small plate. She then served him and sat across from him with hers.

"No ice cream for you?" he asked.

"I love ice cream, but I love it in a dish with lots and lots of chocolate syrup on top. I don't like ice cream with my pie." She looked stricken for a moment. "Oh, I didn't even think about coffee." She half rose from the table but he waved her back down.

"Relax, Marisa, I don't really do coffee this late in the evening," he said.

"Me, neither, unless it's decaffeinated. Sleep is hard enough for me to come by without adding a dose of caffeine before bed."

He took a bite of the pie. The flavor of apples and cinnamon and buttery crust exploded in his mouth. "Oh my gosh, this is one of the best apple pies I've ever tasted." He smiled at her. "You definitely know how to make a pie. Do you cook everything as well as you can make a pie?"

"I used to really enjoy cooking and I like to think I was pretty good at it. When I was living in Oklahoma City one of the things I enjoyed was having dinner parties for my girlfriends."

"What is your specialty?"

She frowned and took a bite of her pie. "I'm not sure I really had one, but if I had to say what I enjoyed cooking the most it was just down-home cooking…maybe a glazed ham with a side of fried potatoes and baked mac and cheese… Things like that."

"Definitely my kind of eating," he replied. "But you're saying everything in the past tense. You don't cook anymore?"

"Not like that. I lost my girlfriends after…after what happened to me and now it just seems like too much trouble to cook like that for myself," she said.

"If you want me to put on a dress and wig and pretend to be one of your girlfriends, I'll do it if you cook that way for me," he said teasingly.

Her laughter filled the room and wrapped around Mac's heart. "It would be almost worth it just to see you in a dress," she finally managed to say.

Then she sobered and looked down at her plate. When she gazed up again, her eyes held a softness he hadn't seen before. "I know you're only here to work with Spirit, but I'm enjoying my time with you, Mac. You relax me with your music and conversation and you've helped me find some of my laughter once again."

Her words touched him and stirred the desire he had to fight against every time they were together. "Marisa, I like spending my time with you, too."

She propped her elbow up on the table, rested her chin in her palm and gazed at him unabashedly. "Why aren't you married, Mac? I would think most of the single women in town would be eager to catch a guy like you."

He released a small laugh and shook his head. "I don't know about all that. I'll admit I've dated a lot in the past, but I've just never found that special woman with whom I want to share my life and my dreams."

"And what dreams are those?"

She didn't seem to be just making idle conversation. She really wanted to know and he wasn't going to just flip out a trite answer, although his adult dreams had certainly been very traditional ones.

"When I first left my father's house, my dream was to get a new guitar and join a band. I was going to show my father by becoming super famous. My band would play huge venues and women fans would throw flowers and their underwear to the stage." He laughed. "Ah, the dreams of a young boy."

"Still, you're good enough at playing and singing to be on stage," she commented.

"Thanks, but as I got older, my dreams changed. Once I got to Cass's ranch I couldn't imagine leaving it for any fleeting fame and fortune I might find. I wanted what most people dreamed about… a soul mate, some babies and my own place. I dreamed of playing to my family and singing lullabies to my babies before they went to bed." He shrugged. "And then about a year ago or so I put that dream away and figured it just wasn't going to happen for me."

He took another bite of his pie and then continued, "Here I am, doing all the talking. What about you, Marisa? What kind of dreams for the future do you have for yourself?"

Surely she didn't intend to live out here, isolated and all alone for the rest of her life? She was far too beautiful, far too young and filled with life to stay locked away here forever.

She looked down at her pie and gazed back at him. Her eyes were dark and flat. "I don't have dreams for my future…not anymore."

He put down his fork and stared at her. "Oh, Marisa, that absolutely breaks my heart for you," he said softly.

"Don't be sad for me, Mac. Who knows what the future might hold. Maybe I'll discover some new dreams for myself with some time."

"I certainly hope so." Their gazes remained locked for several long moments and then she looked back down at her plate. As they finished up the pie their conversation was once again about the weather and Spirit.

But Mac was still upset by what she'd told him about having no dreams for herself. It was obvious to him that she still carried a lot of emotional scars from the crime that had been perpetrated against her. He couldn't help being curious about what exactly she'd been through.

"Why don't you take the rest of this pie with you?" she said as they got up from the table.

"Oh no, I don't want to do that. I don't even have a place to keep it in my room at the ranch. Why don't you just keep it here and if you invite me in again, I'll have another piece."

She gave him one of her elusive, radiant smiles. "I like that idea."

"Me, too." Oh, when she smiled at him that way his heart stuttered its beat and a heat of desire welled up inside him.

She walked with him to the door. When he turned to tell her good-night she stood so close that the fire inside him burned hotter.

"Marisa… I'd like to kiss you." The words fell from him before he realized he was going to say them aloud. However, the minute he'd spoken them he felt sure he didn't want to take them back.

Her eyes flashed and she took a step closer to him. "I'd like you to kiss me, Mac."

She raised her face and her lips opened slightly. Mac's heartbeat accelerated as he took what she offered. He leaned down and captured her mouth with his. She tasted of apples and cinnamon and sweet, hot desire.

She raised her arms to encircle his neck and he placed his hands on her hips and pulled her a little closer. Her lips were so soft and holding her so close fired a welcome heat inside him. He would have liked to bring her even closer to him, to feel how neatly she fit against him, but he refrained in fear that he might make a move she didn't want or wasn't ready for.

Her scent eddied in his head, half dizzying him, and it was only when she dropped her arms from around his neck that he released her and stepped back.

"Good night, Mac," she said softly.

"Good night, Marisa." He turned and stepped out into the night, as always reluctant to say good-bye.

As he drove back to the ranch, his head was not only filled with the taste of her lips, but also with thoughts of the woman herself.

The kiss had been beyond amazing and he definitely wanted to kiss her again...and again. As much as he'd enjoyed tasting her lips, he'd been equally pleased by how open and warm she had been.

He definitely hadn't seen this coming—this magnetic pull toward her. He hadn't realized on that first night when she'd stuck a gun barrel in his back that he would develop such a wealth of feelings for her. And they had come on so fast... like a speeding bullet right into his very heart.

Even though she hadn't shared much with him, he admired her strength, and he hurt for whatever had happened to her. He was learning so much about her as a person...about who she had been before she'd been kidnapped, and he hoped she could claim some of that back again.

No, he hadn't seen this coming at all, but the truth was his heart was getting very involved with her.

He hoped that while he was attempting to gentle Spirit, he was somehow gentling Marisa at the same time. He wanted to take the wildness and distrust from the horse, but he really wished he could do that with the woman, as well.

It would just be his luck that he would help Marisa with her transition back into her best life ever and then she would find another man to fall in love with and marry.

She definitely wouldn't see him coming.

He sat in the basement of the old, run-down

house he owned at the edge of town and stared at the photo of Marisa he'd taken while she was walking down Main Street.

She was even more beautiful now than she'd been years ago. There was a time when he'd dreamed about her. He'd gone to bed every night with thoughts of her in his mind. He'd loved her with a single-minded purpose that had utterly consumed his life.

But she had never *seen* him. He'd tried to talk to her, but she had always been too busy to hear him. She had been part of the snobby, popular crowd. She only dated members of the football team…the golden boys of the school. She hadn't had time to hear or see anyone else.

Eventually his deep love for her had transformed into an all-consuming hatred. He'd been patient. He had waited years, and in those years he had prepared his lair.

Thankfully, the house was fairly isolated and most people thought it was deserted. It had taken him years to think about and plan his course of revenge.

The first time he'd had her captive, he'd been beside himself with excitement. Tormenting her… humiliating her had fed his very soul. And now he knew exactly where she was. He'd initially thought she was staying in her mother's house.

But he now knew she was living in the small

old foreman's cabin deep in a pasture. Now he knew exactly where to find her again. His blood fired through his veins and a rush of adrenaline flowed through him.

He stared at her photo and remembered the last time he'd had her in his lair. It had been so powerful to scare her, to completely humiliate her. He'd watched her scrabbling naked across the floor to find a cheese sandwich he'd thrown in. Her cries for help, her screams of terror had thrilled him.

He needed to punish her for being impervious in not seeing his love for her, for being so high and mighty.

Her final judgment was coming. It was going to be a piece of cake to get her out of that isolated cabin and into his grasp once again.

Oh, he couldn't wait.

And she would never see him coming.

It had been a little over three weeks since Mac had started working with Marisa's horse. Spirit was making really good progress. The night before, the horse had actually gotten close enough to Mac to take the apple from his hand, although she'd shied away at the very last minute before taking it.

Equally important to Spirit's progress was the closeness Marisa was feeling for the handsome cowboy. She found herself anxiously awaiting his arrival each evening and dreading when it was time for him to leave.

She enjoyed his company. The easy way he had about him calmed the screaming demons inside her to a whisper. More than anything, she'd come to trust him completely. She knew he didn't gossip about her or the time they spent together. If he was a gossiper she would have known it by now.

They had kissed a couple more times since the first time and her desire to be with him more intimately had grown to a fever pitch, but first she was planning on telling him about the sixty days of torture.

She had never spoken to anyone about those days except the Oklahoma City detectives who were investigating the case and then to Dillon Bowie, who had also worked on her case from here in Bitterroot. She now found herself ready and wanting to share with Mac.

During the last three weeks she'd learned so much more about him and his life. She'd found out that occasionally he played with a group called the Croakin' Frogs Band at The Watering Hole but he really enjoyed playing for his fellow cowboys at the end of a long day.

She'd learned more about his everyday life at the Holiday ranch and the variety of chores he did there. She also knew that he was fiercely loyal to all the men there, including the new hires who had joined over the last year or two. He had all the qualities she found attractive in a man.

It was Friday once again and she knew Mac had the day off the next day. That would give them more time this evening for maybe taking the relationship to the next level. A shiver raced up her spine as she thought about getting intimate with him. If she decided to follow her instincts, that would happen, but she'd have to see how she felt when the time actually came.

At five thirty she set out the chairs by the corral, and a new shiver of warmth swept through her as she thought of the night to come.

She wanted Mac's touch on her naked skin and she was surprised by her own desire. Maybe he was her experiment to see if she could be that vulnerable with anyone again.

Thankfully, her captor hadn't raped her. At least she hadn't suffered that heinous crime. In any case, she hadn't come away from her experience believing all men were bad. A bad man had taken her, but that didn't mean there weren't any good men.

And she was certain Mac was one of the good guys. After a month of working with him and talking to him every day, she believed she knew the goodness of his heart…of his very soul.

That was why she intended to trust him with everything tonight. She was going to open up her

soul to him… She was going to tell him everything, well, almost everything. She reached down
and stroked Buddy's fur. The dog stretched and
looked up at her with what appeared to be a smile.

Mac and Buddy had become good friends.
Mac petted him and talked to him and the dog
responded well to him. But Marisa knew it would
only take one word from her, one threatening
move by Mac, and Buddy would attack him. Her
safety was Buddy's job.

She heard the horse hooves first. Buddy sat
up and growled menacingly as a man on horseback came riding up. Marisa stood and as he drew
closer she recognized him.

Brendon Timber. He was her old high school
acquaintance and the man who worked the ranch
for her mother. In all the time she'd lived out here,
she had never seen him. The property around the
cabin wasn't part of the Lindale pastureland, although it was still Lindale land.

Brendon was a tall man, with lanky arms and
legs. His brown cowboy hat sat at a cocky angle
on his head, exposing thick blond hair. He had
been a star basketball player in high school, and
with his blond hair, blue eyes and gregarious per-
sonality, he'd never wanted for female attention.

He reined in and offered her a wide smile. "Hi,
Marisa."

"Hi, Brendon." Buddy continued to growl at her

side. She touched the top of his head. "It's okay," she said to the dog. He stopped his growling but remained on his feet at her side. Marisa remained on guard, as well.

Brendon dismounted from the horse. "I can't believe you've been living out here for a while now and I didn't even know it."

"There's no reason why you would have known. This isn't part of the ranch you take care of," Marisa said.

"True," he agreed. He took a step closer to her. "I've got to say, Marisa, you are as pretty as ever."

Her cheeks warmed with the compliment. "Thanks, Brendon."

"I just wanted to stop by and say hello. You know, if you ever need anything out here, I'm here on the property six days a week. Why don't you take my phone number?"

She pulled her phone from her pocket and they exchanged numbers.

"So, are you comfortable out here all by yourself?" Brendon asked.

"I'm not all by myself. I have Buddy to keep me company." She leaned down and patted Buddy's side.

"Yeah, but surely you get lonely for human interaction?"

"I get human interaction whenever I go into town. I'm really quite comfortable here."

"I kind of get it," he replied. "When I got my divorce I enjoyed being alone for a while."

"Oh, I didn't realize you'd been married."

He nodded. "I married Lori Smithton about a year after graduation. We were married almost three years before she started cheating on me. So we wound up getting a divorce."

"I'm sorry to hear that," she replied.

He shrugged. "Thanks, but it was a while ago. It just means I'm back on the market again."

They both turned at the sound of Mac's truck approaching. "What's he doing here?" Brendon asked as Mac pulled up and parked in front of the corral.

"He's a friend and he's been working with my horse," she replied.

Mac got out of his truck with his guitar case in his hand. "Brendon," he said with a nod.

"Hey, Mac," Brendon replied.

Mac shot a glance at her, as if checking to see that she was okay. She gave him a half smile and nodded her head to let him know she was fine.

"Well, I know you're here to work so I'll just be on my way," Brendon said. He remounted his horse. "Don't forget, Marisa. I'm only a phone call away if you ever need anything."

"Thank you, Brendon," she replied. "I appreciate it."

The two men said their goodbyes and then

Brendon galloped off. "You okay?" Mac asked immediately.

"I'm good," she said and returned to her chair. Buddy settled back into the grass next to her. "Brendon just stopped by to say hello."

He sank into the chair next to her and smiled. "I imagine every single man in town will be stopping by to see you now that they all know you're here. I'm sure they're all working up their courage to come out here and woo you."

"It would be a waste of their time. I'm not interested in developing a romantic relationship with anyone," she replied firmly.

She could have sworn she saw a flash of disappointment in his eyes, but then he pulled his guitar out of the case and began to play.

As always she gave herself to his music, letting the notes sing through her soul and smooth all her anger, all her anxiety away. When he added his rich voice to the guitar she closed her eyes.

She could have listened to him all night. She wished she could listen to him every night before she went to bed and have his music and his deep, smooth voice in her head to battle any nightmares that might try to present themselves to her.

Unfortunately, he only sang two songs and then put the guitar away. "Let's see if she'll take the apple tonight," he said.

They got up and went into the corral. He pulled

the apple from his jacket pocket but instead of holding it out before him, he held it out to her. "I think it's time you offered this to Spirit. Maybe she'll take it from you."

Marisa took the apple from him and held it out toward the horse. "Now sweet-talk her," Mac instructed.

"Spirit, you're such a beautiful girl. Come on, girl, you can trust me. I would never hurt you. This apple is nice and juicy and just for you."

The horse sniffed the air and took a step toward her. "Keep talking to her," Mac said softly.

"Come on, Spirit…you can trust us. You can trust me, girl." She desperately wanted to build a loving, forever kind of bond with the horse. "Come on, sweet girl."

Spirit's long-lashed brown eyes reminded her of Mac's. She held Spirit's gaze and felt as if the animal was looking deep into her soul. Marisa desperately wanted the mare to find her trustworthy.

And then Spirit took a couple of quick steps forward and snatched the apple from her hand. An intense thrill rushed through Marisa even as Spirit quickly retreated to the far side of the corral and crunched the apple.

She turned to look at Mac, who grinned at her. "Congratulations," he said. "Now, that's a definite step in the right direction. Let's just hang out right here for a few minutes longer."

"I'm just so excited that she took the apple from me. I feel like singing and dancing," she replied.

Mac laughed. "Save your celebration until we get out of the corral."

They remained in the corral for another fifteen minutes or so. Spirit ate the apple and then took a couple of steps closer to them, as if waiting for them to offer her another treat.

Marisa somehow believed Spirit trusting her enough to take the apple was a sign that it was time she trusted Mac with the knowledge of exactly what had happened to her during those sixty days of hell.

For the first time since that event, she wanted to talk about it. She hoped that if she talked about it out in the open with Mac, then it might finally stop haunting her dreams.

And yet there was still a fear inside her, a fear that somehow in telling she might be judged. Mac might deem her too horribly damaged to continue any kind of a relationship with. She didn't care much about what others thought of her, but it mattered what Mac thought of her, and that scared her more than anything.

Still, she wanted to tell him what she'd endured during those sixty days. She wanted him to understand who she had become, because of her captivity.

Once they'd stored away the chairs in the shed,

she invited him in. "I feel like we need to do something special to celebrate."

"I'll turn on a tune on my phone and we can dance," Mac said.

She smiled at him. "Actually, I think I'd rather just talk."

"That works for me, too," he replied.

He stored his guitar in his truck and then together they went into the cabin, where she immediately took off her gun belt and placed it on the table.

He sank down on the love seat. Normally she sat in the chair opposite him, but tonight she sat next to him.

She was immediately engulfed by his body warmth and his familiar scent. His soft brown eyes invited her in and for the next few minutes they talked about their success with Spirit and what would come next in her training. Then she felt emotionally ready to share with him her most horrid nightmares.

"I'm sure you've wondered why a strong, independent woman like me is so afraid of the dark," she began.

"A lot of people are afraid of the dark," he said, obviously trying to put her at ease. It was one of the qualities she liked about him…his need to make sure she felt comfortable.

"For sixty days I was kept in total darkness."

Mac immediately stilled and then he reached out and took one of her hands in his. His big, slightly calloused hand wrapped around hers in warmth. The connection gave her the strength to continue.

"One minute I was sitting in my car to head out to spend time with a bunch of my coworkers and friends. The next minute I was waking up in a strange, dark place."

She swallowed against the lump of fear that rose up in the back of her throat as she remembered that initial shock of waking up in the dark. "The only thing I knew was that I was naked and on some kind of a mattress on the floor."

She paused to draw a deep breath before continuing. "Once I got over the utter horror and the lingering effects of whatever drug had been used on me, I got up to explore the space. It was a small room. I used my hands to search every area, desperate to find a way out. I finally found a door, but it was locked and no light came in around it. The only other thing in the room was a bucket. I screamed for help, I screamed until I was hoarse, but needless to say nobody came to help me."

She paused for a long moment, her muscles tensing, and took a couple of deep breaths. Mac gently squeezed her hand, as if giving her the strength to go on. His brown eyes held nothing but a wealth of compassion.

"That's when all the strangeness started. Whoever held me hostage began to poke at me with what felt like a stick. I know it sounds rather benign, but it was absolutely terrifying. I never knew when or where I'd be poked and all of it happened in darkness. There were times when I would think I was alone in the room and then my hair would be pulled by somebody."

"I can definitely see that being terrifying," Mac said softly.

"And then there were times I knew he was in the room with me." This time she squeezed Mac's hand. "He'd grab at me and laugh when I screamed. He had to be wearing some sort of goggles or glasses that allowed him to see in the dark. But I couldn't see him. I'd feel his hot breath on my neck or his hand in my hair or on my shoulder and I was absolutely terrified."

There was no way to explain the utter terror of being trapped in a room with somebody who could see you, but you couldn't see. It was sheer terror to be naked and vulnerable in a room where a man chased you around in the dark.

"The worst part of it all was the not knowing exactly what he was capable of. Was he going to rape me? Kill me? I had no idea what might happen next." A shiver worked up her spine in response to her horrible memories.

"Did…did he rape you?" Mac's eyes were so warm, so filled with tender caring.

"No…at least not that I'm aware of, but one day I was drugged and when I woke I was blindfolded and tied down to some kind of a hard table. I heard a buzzing sound and it took me only a minute to realize he was tattooing my hip."

One of Mac's brows rose. "What in the hell did he tattoo on you?"

"'You're mine.' Those were the words. Since then I had it tattooed over and I now have a very large flower there. After he did that to me, my terror was even greater." A deep breath fluttered out of her.

"I'm so sorry, Marisa. My sweet Marisa," he murmured.

She loved the sound of her name falling from his lips, and with his solid warmth and support right next to her, she continued to share with him the details of her captivity.

She told him about the horror of the complete darkness and of being touched and prodded. She was fed by her captor throwing in a paper-wrapped sandwich and a bottle of water. She'd have to crawl around on the floor to find those items. She explained the terror of how the uncertainty and lack of control over anything weighed heavily on her.

She was able to discern day from night only

once she realized there was a pattern to the assaults. Hours would pass where nothing happened. Then she'd hear footsteps on the floor above her and know he was back and the tormenting would begin all over again.

Now, to her horror, she began to weep. No matter how hard she tried to contain the tears, she couldn't, as she remembered that time of uncertainty and fear. Mac instantly pulled her into his arms and held her. He stroked down her back and whispered words of encouragement and of caring.

That only made her cry harder because she hadn't realized until now how badly she had needed somebody to whisper in her ear and tell her she was okay and that none of what had happened was her fault. She hadn't recognized until this very moment that she had needed big strong arms to surround her and hold her tight. She'd needed Mac's arms around her.

She didn't know how long she cried, but finally the tears subsided. Still she remained leaned into Mac with her face pressed against his broad chest.

"He promised he'd come for me again," she whispered. "The last words he said to me was a vow that he'd catch me again and the next time he'd never let me go." She finally sat up and looked at Mac.

"Does he know you're from Bitterroot?" Mac asked.

"Not only does he know, but he told me he was also from Bitterroot," she replied.

Mac looked at her in surprise. "I'd just assumed he was from Oklahoma City. How do you know he was telling you the truth about being from Bitterroot?"

"He knew things about the town that only a native would know. He knew about the kissing tree on the Miller property."

It was a tree all the high school kids knew about. When a couple kissed beneath the tree and carved their initials into the trunk, they were supposed to be assured of a happily-ever-after together.

"But it doesn't really matter where he was from. He told me no matter where I went he would find me. I figured if what he said was true, then I might as well move back here."

Mac frowned. "Do you have any idea at all who it might be?"

She shook her head. "Not a clue. I never saw him at all and I knew he was disguising his voice every time he talked to me. I don't even have a clue about his general body size."

"Do you really think he'll come back for you?" His eyes were dark and troubled.

There was no way she was willing to share with him that she hoped the madman would come back for her, that she was really hoping to kill him. She cared about Mac, but she didn't want him to try to play her hero.

She didn't need a hero.

"No, I really don't think he'll come for me again." She hated to lie to Mac, but this was a lie to keep him safe. "I think he was just saying that to scare me. He'd be a fool to try it twice. Besides, there are days I'm really not even sure he's really from Bitterroot at all," she said, contradicting herself from only moments before. "And now I don't want to talk about any of this anymore. This night was supposed to be a celebration."

"Marisa, thank you for sharing with me. I can't imagine how horrible that time was for you. I'm just so damned sorry this happened to you. You didn't deserve that." He held her gaze for a long moment and then he offered her his warm and comforting smile. "Okay, now what do you have in mind for a celebration?"

His words and his reaction to what she had just told him made her certain of what she now wanted. "How about we start with a kiss?" She saw her words had shocked him, but his eyes immediately darkened and a slow smile curved his lips.

"Far be it from me to deny a beautiful woman." He leaned forward and gently captured her lips with his.

She wound her arms around his neck and then

she was the one who leaned in and deepened the kiss. She wanted him. She'd already been vulnerable enough to share her sixty-day story with him. She'd already been vulnerable enough to cry in his arms. Now she was ready to give herself to him fully, in a different way.

His kiss fired a sizzling heat through her. His lips were soft but held a masterful command that made it impossible to deny. When she opened her mouth their tongues swirled together and the fire inside her shot higher.

When the kiss finally ended, she took his hand in hers and stood. "Mac, I want you to make love with me."

She expected him to eagerly jump up from the love seat, but instead he remained in place and held her gaze. "Marisa, are you sure that's really what you want? It's been a pretty emotional night. I don't want this to be just a whim that you'll regret in the morning."

"Trust me, I won't regret it as long as you understand that I'm not looking for love or forever. However, I'm very sure about wanting you tonight, Mac."

She was so certain of what she wanted that she'd gone to the drugstore earlier in the day and had bought condoms. Thankfully, nobody else had been in the pharmacy and she hadn't known the woman cashier. She certainly didn't want that kind of gossip floating around town.

She tugged on his hand once again and this time he stood and pulled her into a tight embrace. His lips took hers again, this time in a kiss that created a new flame deep in her veins.

When the kiss finally ended, together they walked into her bedroom. Buddy attempted to follow them, but she stopped him with a single command. "Guard." Buddy immediately moved to the center of the living room and sat.

She closed the bedroom door and then looked at the rugged, handsome cowboy before her. His desire for her shone bright in his eyes and her own need to be held, to be touched and made love to torched through her.

Without saying a word she sat on the edge of the bed and pulled off her boots and socks. He mimicked her actions, apparently okay to let her take the lead.

She stood from the bed and walked over to where he now stood. When she placed her fingers on the top button of his flannel shirt, she heard his swift intake of breath. He stood still and didn't utter a word as she slowly unbuttoned his shirt and then pushed it off his shoulders and to the floor behind him. She then grabbed the bottom of his white undershirt and with his help pulled it up and over his head.

Mac's chest was splendid…broad and muscled with just a smattering of hair in the center that narrowed as it disappeared into the top of his jeans. She couldn't help but run her hands across the muscled expanse. Once again he tensed and sucked in his breath at her touch.

His skin was so warm and his shoulders so broad, as if the weight of the world could sit on top and he'd be able to handle it.

She stepped back from him and drew her sweater over her head, leaving her in a lacy black bra. The hunger that shone from his eyes as he looked at her half dizzied her.

While she took off her leggings, he took off his jeans. Even though he had black boxers beneath, it was obvious that he was very aroused.

His heated gaze swept down her body, feeling like a physical caress. "Marisa, you are so beautiful," he half whispered.

"So are you." Mac had the perfect physique… broad shoulders and a lean stomach, slender hips and long, athletic legs.

She pulled down the bedspread, slid beneath the sheets and beckoned him to join her there. He quickly got into the bed and pulled her toward him for another deep kiss. When the kiss ended, she stroked her fingers down the side of his face.

"I know most people make love in the dark, but I need the lights on," she said.

He smiled at her with obvious understanding. "I like the lights on. This way I can see your gorgeous face while we make love."

He framed her face with his hands and then gave her a sweet, gentle kiss.

Marisa's heart stirred in a way it never had before. It swelled in her chest, nearly taking her breath away. Mac seemed to be the perfect lover for her. He didn't mind the light that she so desperately needed.

Surely she wasn't falling in love with Mac? She couldn't. Love had nothing to do with her future plans.

Still, for this night and in this moment she intended to shove that troubling thought aside and fully give herself to him.

Chapter 6

Mac was on fire. As he kissed and caressed Marisa, his desire for her was something he'd never experienced before with any other woman. Her scent surrounded him and half dizzied him. He'd never been so turned on.

She was an eager and willing participant. As he explored her body with his hands, she did the same to his. Their kisses grew more frantic and he loved that he could see her need for him shining from her gorgeous eyes.

After several minutes she reached around and unfastened her bra. Her breasts were small, but absolutely exquisite. He immediately began to lick and tease her nipples while her fingers tangled in his hair and she released a deep moan.

As he plied her breasts with his tongue, he moved one hand down her stomach and to the black panties she had on. He wanted to give her as much pleasure as he could before he took his own. He knew the minute he entered her he wouldn't be able to last long at all. He'd been on a slow burn for her for too long already.

She arched up to meet his touch and he took the opportunity to pull her panties down and off her slender hips. He returned to moving his fingers against her. He felt the growing tension in her body and wanted to take her to the edge and over. She grasped his shoulders, her gaze burning into his.

"Don't stop," she whispered, her voice filled with tense need.

In answer to her, he increased the pressure and quickness of his fingers against her. Then she was there…she closed her eyes, tensed and moaned over and over again as he felt the shudders of her orgasm rushing through her.

When she opened her eyes, they shone with a new hunger. "More," she whispered. "I want more, Mac."

She reached down and shoved at his boxers to take them off him. When they were off, her warm hand encircled his throbbing hardness. He nearly lost it. He shoved her hand away. "Marisa, you can't touch me like that if you want more," he said.

She rolled over and grabbed a condom from her dresser. "How about if I touch you like this?" She opened the packet and tossed it aside and then slowly rolled the condom on his length, sending him half-mad with his desire.

Within seconds he was positioned between her thighs and he slowly entered her. With her urging, he buried himself in her moist heat. He paused for a long moment, simply savoring the overwhelming sensations that rushed through him.

As he began to move inside her, he leaned down and kissed her. When the kiss ended, their gazes remained locked. Her eyes were more blue than gray and he felt as if she was attempting to look into his very soul. The eye contact made the whole act feel even more intimate.

Faster and faster they moved together. Once again he felt her climbing…climbing…and when she climaxed again, he came with her and moaned her name over and over again.

When it was all over, they both rolled onto their backs as they tried to catch their breaths. He finally turned and propped himself up on one elbow. He smiled down at her. "That was…was…" He sought for the perfect word.

"Amazing," she replied with one of her beautiful smiles.

"Even better than amazing," he said.

"Fantastical," she offered.

He laughed. "Super fantastical." He sobered and leaned over and ran his fingers over the red-and-black flower that decorated her hip. It was a beautiful tattoo, but knowing why it was there and what it hid broke his heart.

"I thought about getting a skull and crossbones tattooed over it," she said. "But then I decided I needed to create something beautiful there."

"The flower is beautiful," he said. "You are beautiful."

She laughed. "Said the man who is sexually sated."

"You know that's not why I'm telling you that you're beautiful. You are beautiful not just on the outside, but also on the inside. I can't believe how strong you are and how you've survived so much with dignity and grace."

"Don't give me too much credit, Mac," she replied.

He gazed at her for a long moment and then gave her a kiss that he hoped held all the tenderness, all the love he had in his heart for her. When the kiss ended, he swung his legs over the side of the bed and stood.

"Buddy won't eat me when I step out of the bedroom, will he?" he asked.

"Only if I tell him to," she assured him and

then she giggled. It was such a girlish, wonderful sound it wrapped itself tight around his heart.

When he stepped out of the bedroom, Buddy merely gazed at him. Mac went into the small bathroom and quickly cleaned himself up and then went back into the bedroom.

He sat on the edge of the bed and reached for his boxers and jeans. "Mac." Her soft voice caused him to turn and face her. "Stay with me tonight?"

He dropped his clothes back to the floor and returned to the bed. He immediately pulled her into his arms and she relaxed against him. "Now, this is what I call a celebration," she said softly.

He laughed. "You certainly won't get an argument from me."

"Thank you for letting me tell you everything about my sixty days of hell," she said.

He reached out and ran his index finger down the side of her beautiful face. "Thank you for trusting me enough to tell me. Have you ever spoken about it to anyone other than law enforcement?"

"I was in therapy for a couple of months right after, but that's not the same as telling a friend," she replied.

"I'm glad you consider me your friend." Although he certainly didn't intend to share with his friends what he and Marisa had just shared in bed. He definitely wouldn't breathe a word to anyone about her sixty days in hell. He also hoped to become much more than a friend to her.

"Will the lights bother you to sleep?" she asked, her voice getting drowsy.

"Marisa, trust me, nothing is going to bother me tonight," he replied.

However, two hours later, long after she had fallen asleep, Mac remained awake. It wasn't necessarily the bright illumination in the room that kept him awake, but rather everything she had told him earlier in the evening.

Something about what she'd said was confusing. As he went over everything she had told him, his confusion increased. If she believed the perp who had kidnapped her before might come after her again, then why on earth had she chosen to live in this isolated cabin?

Surely no matter how badly she got along with her mother, her mother wouldn't want her to be in any danger. Why hadn't Marisa moved into the big house with her? Or why not get an apartment in town, where she would be around other people?

Then she had told him she didn't think the perp was from Bitterroot at all and she didn't believe he would come after her again. That was where her story made less sense.

Her horrific tale of her sixty days in captivity had broken his heart for her. He couldn't imagine the humiliation of her nakedness, the deprivation of light and the sheer terror she'd been through.

He couldn't believe that he was here with her now, in her bed after making love. He was so happy that she'd trusted him enough not only to share her trauma, but also enough to share herself intimately with him.

However, he sensed she still had secrets... dark secrets that troubled him. He cared about her deeply and the last thing he wanted was for anything bad to ever happen to her again.

He must have finally fallen asleep. When he awakened, despite the blackout curtains at the windows, his body clock told him it was early morning.

Marisa was snuggled against his side and still asleep. He took the opportunity to study her features. She was even more beautiful than she had been ten years ago, when she'd been a homecoming queen and voted Miss Bitterroot at the fall festival. She had been a girl then, but she was all woman now.

Her shiny black hair back then had been long and flowing around her shoulders, but the short cut she now wore suited her delicate features. Her skin was flawless and her eyelashes were long and thick.

Their sleepy bodies had found each other in the middle of the night and they had made love a second time. It had been slower, less frantic than the first time, but just as wonderful.

Her eyes suddenly snapped open. She stared at him for a long moment and then smiled and said, "Good morning." She moved away from him and stretched like a contented cat.

"Good morning to you," he replied.

She sat up. "Want some breakfast?"

"Sure." Today was his day off, so he had all the time in the world to linger as long as she wanted him to. She got out of bed and he did the same. She grabbed some clothes from the dresser and then turned back to him. "I'll meet you in the kitchen."

Once she left the room Mac picked his clothes up from where they had fallen the night before and got dressed. He pulled the blankets back up on the bed and straightened the pillows and by that time the scent of coffee brewing let him know she was already dressed and in the kitchen area.

Buddy greeted him when he stepped out of the bedroom. He pressed his nose into Mac's hand, obviously looking for some loving. "Hey, Buddy," Mac said and scratched the top of the dog's head. "Did you get lonely last night, big guy?"

Marisa stood at the stove. "Coffee will be ready in just a few minutes. Why don't you sit and relax? I hope you like bacon and eggs."

"I love bacon and eggs," he replied. "Are you sure I can't do anything to help?"

She smiled at him. "With this kitchen area being so small, the best thing you can do right now is sit and stay out of my way."

"Got it." He sat at the table and Buddy sank down at his feet.

For a few minutes they remained silent and Mac wondered if she was feeling any awkwardness after what had happened between them the night before. He didn't feel awkward, but he didn't want to say or do anything that might create any tension. He just hoped she didn't have any regrets this morning.

"How do you like your coffee?" she asked as she poured two cups.

"Black is fine."

"Same with me," she replied. She delivered his cup to the table. "How did you sleep?"

"Like a log," he replied. "What about you?"

She grinned at him. "Same with me. So the lights on didn't bother you?"

"Not at all. I can sleep with the lights off or on, the television playing or not playing, and with a storm blowing wind and rain against the window."

"I'm just glad I didn't have a nightmare last night." She returned to the oven to turn over the bacon. "I was afraid I might have one after talking about everything."

"Do you have nightmares often?" he asked and then took a sip of his coffee.

"Not every night, but often enough. Usually Buddy wakes me by licking my face and whining."

Mac's heart constricted with the idea of her having a nightmare and having nobody beside her except a loving dog. If he could, he'd be here every night so that if she had a nightmare he could pull her close to him and soothe her. He'd hold her tight and make her feel loved and protected and keep her away from her dark, nighttime demons.

However, she wasn't inviting him to move in here with her. She had specifically told him she wasn't looking for a relationship. He was really just a man working with her horse whom she had invited in for a night of sex. For some reason this thought depressed him more than a little bit.

Over breakfast they talked about Spirit's progress and the approach of winter. "Thank goodness I have plenty of firewood to get me through the winter months, since the only heat source in this place is the fireplace," she said.

"Where do you get your wood?" he asked.

"I ordered two cords from Jake Mosby a couple of months ago."

"Now, there's a strange bird," Mac said. "When we were all growing up we were sure Jake lived up in a tree and ate little kids for lunch."

Marisa laughed. "My friends had the same kind of thoughts about him. We were sure he was some sort of a warlock who could become any wild animal he wanted to be."

"And he's really just a cranky old man who lives in a cabin in the woods and prefers to commune with nature rather than people." Mac shook his head with another laugh. "It's amazing what kind of boogeymen kids can come up with."

"But not all boogeymen are just figments of young minds," she replied, and for a moment her gaze darkened.

"Marisa, why are you living out here all alone?" he asked once she was seated across from him with their breakfast before them. "Why not get a place in town where there are more people around?"

"First of all if I was living in town I wouldn't be able to keep Spirit," she replied.

He looked at her with a touch of disbelief. "I'm sure your mother wouldn't mind stabling Spirit and letting her stay here where you could come every day to visit with her," he said.

She frowned and took a drink of her coffee before replying. "When I first moved back to Bitterroot, I wanted to be by myself. I needed the time to heal." She wrapped her fingers around her mug. "Unfortunately I couldn't do that in my mother's house. She is of the mind that I had to have done something wrong to warrant the attention of a stalker. I must have been dressing too sexy or acting too wild. In any case, this cabin now feels like home to me, but who knows what the future holds?"

"You know that nothing you did and no matter how you dressed it wasn't your fault that a stalker came after you."

"On an intellectual level I know that," she said. "I just wish my mother understood that."

"Marisa, I just hope your future doesn't include you staying here in this cabin all alone for the rest of your life. I want you to be happy. You deserve to live a happy and fulfilling life."

She flashed him that quick, beautiful smile. "Thanks, Mac."

They finished eating and then he helped her clear the table. As she washed the dishes, he dried them and put them away in the appropriate cabinets. When the task was all finished, he figured it was time for him to leave. He definitely didn't want to hang around long enough to become an unwanted houseguest.

"Since it's my day off, why don't I plan on being back here around two this afternoon to work with Spirit," he suggested as she walked him to the door.

"That sounds good to me." She opened her front door and leaned toward him with a smile. "Kiss me before you leave?"

"I'd be happy to." He gathered her into his arms

where he felt as if she belonged and then gave her a kiss he hoped would linger in her mind for hours to come. He knew it would linger in his.

When the kiss ended, he released her and she stepped back from him. "Then I'll just see you later," she said with a smile.

They said their goodbyes and he left the cabin and headed for his truck. As crazy as it was, he hadn't wanted to leave. He would have liked to stay with her for days…for weeks…for as long as it took to know her inside and out. He would have liked to stay long enough for her to fall in love with him.

He was definitely falling in love with her, and it wasn't necessarily a happy feeling. Just because she had made love with him last night didn't mean she was falling in love with him.

No, he wasn't happy at all about the way he felt about Marisa. In fact, it had his heartbreak written all over it.

She shouldn't have let him into her bedroom. Even though she'd desperately wanted him, she should have been stronger and resisted her desire for him.

There was no question that she found Mac's presence to be a calm and steadying influence on her. Not only that, but she found him funny and sexy as hell.

She loved the conversations they shared. Sometimes they were light and silly, and other times they were deep and thought-provoking.

He'd been the kind of lover she'd wanted and thought him to be, not only masterful and exciting, but also wonderfully tender and unselfish.

However, she was allowing him to get too close. Worse than her physical longing for him was her desire to get closer to him mentally and emotionally.

Who would really want to be in a relationship with a woman who slept with all the lights on and had Tasers, guns and knives hidden all around her house?

Who would want to love a woman who gave little of herself and was plotting to kill a man? If Mac ever found out how truly dark her soul was, he'd surely run for the hills as any sane man would do.

And if and when she had her final confrontation with the man who had stolen her life, it was possible she'd go to prison. Even if she didn't face any criminal charges at all, she knew that killing a man would change the very core of who she was and how people would forever look at her.

She was far too broken to even consider a relationship with a wonderful man like Mac or any other man. She feared she would always be too broken to love fully or to be loved.

But making love with him had been beyond wonderful. He'd been masterful in his caresses and his touch had shot flames of heat and excitement through her veins.

Even thinking about it now, despite the fact that they'd made love twice last night, as she straightened the love seat cushions, she wanted to do it all over again. She couldn't imagine any other man in her bed, but she could definitely imagine Mac in it once again.

She shoved the thought out of her mind and sank down on the sofa. Buddy stood in front of her, looking at her adoringly. She'd let him outside earlier before she'd made the coffee.

"How are you doing, Buddy boy?" She patted the cushion beside her.

Buddy immediately jumped up next to her and laid his big head on her chest. She stroked her fingers through his thick fur. "Sorry you got kicked out of the bedroom last night, Buddy. I hope you forgive me for needing Mac last night."

His tail thumped as if to let her know he didn't hold a grudge. Her heart swelled with love for the dog. He loved her no matter how broken she was and she knew he would give his very life for her.

She remained on the love seat with Buddy for about half an hour and then got up and went into the bathroom for a shower. Beneath the hot spray of water she once again found herself thinking about the night before with Mac.

She had told him what had happened to her but there was no real way to truly express to another person the utter degradation she'd felt, the abject terror she'd lived with while in the dark for those days.

Nobody had been more surprised than her when she'd awakened after being drugged and had found herself on Main Street in Bitterroot. She had no idea whether she'd been held for those two months in Oklahoma City or in Bitterroot or someplace else altogether.

The Oklahoma City detectives who had worked her case had been frustrated by the lack of clues. Once she was found in Bitterroot they had coordinated their efforts with Dillon Bowie, the chief of police here in the small town. Ultimately, with no more leads and no more clues forthcoming, it had become a cold case.

It wasn't cold for her. The need for retribution burned hot inside her. She knew the rage, the overwhelming need she had would eventually destroy any love she might find with Mac.

She'd just gotten out of the shower and dressed when her phone rang. She froze and stared at the caller identification. It was a number she didn't recognize.

Was it him? Was this the beginning of the end?

Her heart banged in her chest and her stomach twisted in knots. It rang twice more before she finally picked up the phone and answered.

"Marisa, it's Brendon."

Her air whooshed out of her lungs. "Hi, Brendon."

"Hey, I was thinking since it was Saturday night maybe you'd like to go with me to The Watering Hole and have a few drinks? I know it's pretty much last-minute, but I just thought you might want to get out of the cabin and do a little socializing."

"Thanks for the offer, Brendon, but I'm really not going out with anyone right now."

"Not even for a friendly drink?"

"Not even for that," she replied. "But I appreciate you thinking of me."

"Okay, well, let me know if and when you're ready to get out of that cabin and I'll be glad to take you out," he said.

"I'll do that, and once again thanks for the offer."

They said their goodbyes and then she hung up. Brendon and Zeke Osmond were both on her radar. They had shamefully chased her all through high school, but she hadn't been interested in either one of them.

She'd dated Jacob Enderly, the captain of the football team, in high school. However, after graduation he'd moved with his family to California, and eventually she and Jacob had lost touch with each other.

Right now all men in Bitterroot were suspects. The only man she didn't doubt was Mac. Already she was looking forward to seeing him again and that worried her.

At one thirty she set the chairs out next to the corral. As she did, she talked to Spirit. It had been such a thrill the night before when the horse had trusted her enough to take the apple from her. She was hoping the same thing would happen tonight.

Spirit was looking better and better with each day that passed. She'd put on weight and her coat was beginning to shine. She also appeared calmer and Marisa knew that was thanks to Mac.

She, too, felt less agitated whenever she was around Mac. It wasn't just his music and his voice when he sang; he just had a calming effect on her. She had to start fighting against it. She was falling for the man and she couldn't let her feelings toward him get out of control.

She needed a solitary life to bait a man and have him come after her. She didn't want to get close to Mac and somehow slip up by telling him her plan. She knew he would try to stop her and she refused to allow anything or anyone—not even love—to stop her from her plans.

* * *

He'd watched her long enough to know her basic schedule. If she was going to go out during the day, she usually left her cabin before noon and was back home by around two or three.

He'd also seen the German shepherd she owned. He wasn't scared of a dog. For the most part he liked dogs. There were several strays that hung out around his work. Still, as unfortunate as it was, when the time came he could easily take care of it with a little tainted meat or a dart gun filled with poison. He wasn't about to allow some trained animal to keep him from his goal.

Anytime he saw her out walking the streets of Bitterroot or eating lunch in the café his blood boiled. He hated her. She held her head up so high, as if she was so much better than everyone else.

When he remembered having her in his control, he couldn't help smiling. It had been amazing, watching her scrabble naked across the floor in the dark and trying to escape the pole he used to prod her with. She hadn't looked so high and mighty then.

He'd tried to forget about her when high school was over and he heard she'd moved to Oklahoma City, but no matter how hard he tried he couldn't. His hatred of her had eaten him up inside, growing worse and worse as each year had gone by.

He'd found her in Oklahoma City by her website business and within a week he had her home address. It was easy to drive an hour and a half after work and on his days off to stalk her and see when the best time to snatch her might be.

That night he'd just gotten lucky. He'd gotten lucky but he'd also been ready. He'd been sitting in the parking lot of her apartment building when she'd come outside.

As she walked to her car, he'd realized tonight was the night. The time was now. He'd pulled on the black ski mask. Electric currents of adrenaline had shocked through him as he crept out of his car. He'd timed it perfectly. After she half slid into the driver's seat and before she could close her door, he'd jumped into action.

He'd grabbed her, gagged her and drugged her within mere seconds. She'd struggled with him only a few short minutes before the drug worked, and she'd gone limp in his arms.

He'd loaded her in his back seat, knowing she would be out for some time. As he'd driven back to this place in Bitterroot he'd been beside himself with excitement.

Unfortunately he'd only been able to come here in the evenings and on his days off his job, but those nights of humiliating her, of emotionally torturing her were the best nights of his life.

Eventually he'd grown bored with her. He'd thought about killing her, but then he'd come up with a different, better idea, and that was to let her go and then recapture her all over again.

After all, the chase was almost as good as the capture. And it was even better when she knew he was coming and couldn't do a damn thing about it. He liked the idea of her being so afraid even before he got her in his grips.

This time when he got her, he wouldn't let her go. She needed to pay for those high school days when she didn't *see* him, when she was too snobby to see his love for her. She needed to suffer and die for all the tears he'd shed over her.

She reminded him of his mother. Elaine had been a beautiful woman, too. She was too good to spend time with her son. She preferred the company of the gentlemen in town, gentlemen that she whored for.

He couldn't count the number of nights he'd sobbed himself to sleep after being left all alone by his uncaring mother. He'd been nothing but a young child left all alone in a filthy, rat-infested apartment. He'd beg and plead for her to stay home with him, but she never did.

Sometimes the two women, Marisa and his mother, melded together in his mind. But his mother no longer walked the earth. Three years ago she'd had an "accidental" fall down a flight of stairs and had died from the injuries. He hoped she had gone straight to hell.

Still, he'd been watching Marisa and he also knew Mac McBride, one of Big Cass's exalted cowboys, was spending time working with her horse.

He also knew there had been a couple of nights when Mac had spent the night with her. Poor guy. He was pretty certain that she was just toying with him. Marisa Lindale would never be interested in a simple ranch hand. He imagined she still thought she was better than any of the men in Bitterroot.

In fact, he'd just watched Mac leave her place. He hid far enough away from the cabin in a copse of trees where not even the dog got wind of him.

As Mac's truck rumbled by, he thought about going in to take her right now. But he'd come unprepared to take her tonight. He didn't have any way to neutralize the dog or anything to drug her with.

Besides, he needed to start with the phone calls and notes so that she would once again feel the terror before the actual takedown. She would know he was coming, but she wouldn't know when or where.

He was ready and he needed it all to begin again right now.

Chapter 7

Mac had just come home from Marisa's cabin. He entered his room and tossed his hat on the bed and then placed his guitar on a straight-backed chair nearby. He thought about just going to bed, but he was restless with thoughts blowing around in his head like a spring storm.

Instead of getting ready to go to sleep, he decided to go around to the back of the cowboy motel to the rec room.

In the past two weeks, he'd spent the night with Marisa two more times. Each time had been as magical as the first. He wasn't just falling in love with her, he was already there.

He loved Marisa with all his heart and soul. If he believed she was in the same place as he was, he'd be ready to ask her to marry him and spend her life with him.

However, he was pretty sure she wasn't in the same place. Even though they'd made love again and he'd spent those nights with her, she definitely, continually, gave him mixed signals.

There were times when he felt like they were in the same headspace, but there were other times when he sensed her pulling away from him and he didn't know why or what to do about it.

He was just a little bit depressed about it and there was nothing better to help than a little time with some of the other cowboys at the Holiday ranch.

Mac was the only one of the twelve original cowboys who still lived on the ranch. The others had their own homes to go to when the day's work was over.

Tonight there were three men sitting in the room, drinking beer and talking. All three were hardworking, affable men whom Mac liked.

"Hey, Mac," Eric Lee greeted him with a smile.

"Hey, boys, what's going on?" Mac sank down on the sofa next to Brad Adams and across from Eric and Tucker Caldwell.

"Nothing is going on except a little drinking and a whole lot of bull talking," Tucker said with a laugh. "Want a beer?" He gestured to the cooler of ice and beverages at his feet.

"No, thanks, I'm good. So, what were you all talking about?" Mac asked. He wanted any conversation that might get Marisa out of his mind for at least a little while.

"Humes's men and how disrespectful and crappy they always are to all of us anytime we run into them in town," Tucker said.

"Lloyd Green and Zeke Osmond are the absolute worst, but all of them are really hateful," Brad said.

"They've been that way for years," Mac said. Because all three of the men weren't Bitterroot natives and had only recently come here to work on the Holiday ranch, Mac explained some of the history between Raymond Humes and Big Cass.

Years ago, when Cass's husband was dying and she was trying to take care of him and keep the ranch running, Raymond had cornered Cass in her barn and had tried to rape her.

She had managed to get away from him, but not before she'd bullwhipped Raymond on his naked butt. After that Raymond had vowed to destroy her. Even after her death he still had a single goal to destroy the Holiday ranch, and he hated Cassie as much as he had hated her aunt.

"Wow, that's some story," Brad said when Mac was finished.

"Yeah, thanks for giving us the history behind all this," Eric said.

"I hadn't heard any of that before," Tucker added.

"The history doesn't really matter much now. All you really have to know is there's been bad blood with them for years and to expect trouble whenever they're around," Mac said.

"Too bad Dillon hasn't been able to arrest some of them." Brad leaned down and grabbed another beer from the cooler.

"It's got to be really frustrating for him," Mac said. "There are all kinds of mischief and crimes happening on his property and he's been unable to get enough evidence to make a single arrest."

Eric narrowed his gaze. "They are a sneaky bunch. We've already had about a dozen cattle mysteriously disappear from the herd."

"You can bet those cattle are now a part of the Humes herd," Tucker said. "And a bunch of fencing was pulled down this morning between our pasture and theirs."

"I came here to hang out because I was feeling a little low. All this talk about those guys certainly isn't helping with that," Mac said dryly.

"Ah, man, what are you sad about? That horse being difficult and not training the way you want her to?" Brad asked.

"No, the work with the horse has been moving along just great," Mac said.

"So, if it isn't the horse…it must be the woman," Eric said with a knowing twinkle in his eye.

"Don't even try to deny it, Mac. We all know you and Marisa have gotten quite cozy with each other," Brad added.

"To be honest, I'm crazy about her," Mac admitted. He felt a warmth jump into his cheeks. This was the first time he'd confessed to anyone his feelings about Marisa. "But I feel like she's giving me mixed messages," he added.

"Ha, what woman doesn't?" Tucker exclaimed. "One day Suzie tells me she loves me to death and the next day she'll swear that she hates my guts and never wants to see me again."

"Women." Eric shook his head. "Can't live with them, can't live without them."

"I just wish I had one in my life to give me some mixed signals," Brad lamented. "Seems to me like all the women in town I might be interested in have an engagement or wedding ring on their fingers and that's a line I don't cross."

"So, what kind of mixed signals is she giving you?" Eric asked.

Mac frowned. "One minute she's warm and affectionate with me and then the next she withdraws and closes herself off."

"Do you think maybe it has something to do

with whatever she went through when she was kidnapped?" Tucker asked.

"I don't know…maybe," Mac replied. He suddenly realized he didn't really want to talk about Marisa with the other men.

He liked them all and knew they would want to help him. He also believed they would all keep this discussion private between just the four of them. However, there was really no advice they could give him that would make sense in the situation he found himself in.

He was in love with a woman he didn't understand, a woman he still believed had dark secrets that she wasn't willing to share with him…with anyone. One minute he thought he saw love for him shining from her eyes and the next her eyes were tightly shuttered, offering him nothing at all.

He hung out with the other men for another half hour or so and then he stood. "Gentlemen, I believe it's time I called it quits for the night."

Brad got up, as well. "I'm with you, Mac. From the work schedule I saw, I'm going to be mucking out stalls all day tomorrow and staying up half the night won't make that job get any better."

"Ah, lucky you," Eric replied with a wry grin. "We all hate having to muck out the stalls, but it's one of those chores that need to be done."

"And on that note I believe I'm going to finish my beer before heading to bed," Tucker said.

"I'll sit with you for a few more minutes," Eric said to Tucker.

Good-nights were said and then Brad and Mac left the rec room and walked together around to the private rooms. "I guess I'll see you in the morning," Brad said when they reached his room.

"Not tomorrow, it's my day off," Mac replied. "But I'll probably see you for dinner tomorrow night. Good night, Brad."

"Maybe tomorrow night after dinner you'll play a little guitar for us. It's been a minute since we've gotten to enjoy your music."

"I can do that," Mac replied, pleased by Brad's request.

"I'll look forward to that. 'Night, Mac," Brad replied. He disappeared inside and Mac continued on to his own room.

Once inside, he undressed, took a quick shower and then got into bed. This evening when he'd been at Marisa's he'd managed to get a bridle on Spirit and lead her around the corral.

Marisa had been so happy with Spirit's progress she'd thrown her arms around his neck and laughed. She'd danced with him around the corral and kissed his cheek with an exhilaration and excitement that had tripped his heartstrings.

It had been a moment of seeing her free of any dark shadows, of seeing the full potential of the warm and caring woman he believed her to be. It had been positively magical.

He wanted that woman. With each day that passed he wanted her more and more. He just didn't know if that woman wanted him. All he could hope for was that with more time she'd fall in love with him.

Maybe it was time that he told her exactly how he felt about her. Maybe it was time he proclaimed his complete and utter love for her. Tomorrow when he went to work with Spirit maybe he'd do just that.

However, he felt as if he was running out of time. Spirit was now allowing him to hands-on work with her. Within weeks he expected to get on her back and break her in for riding.

Once that happened and he could get Marisa riding, then he would no longer be going to her house every day. Their relationship as horse trainer and client would be over. And he feared any other relationship they'd been building as man and woman could be over, as well.

Once Mac left her place, Marisa had taken a long shower, changed into her nightclothes and then built a roaring fire in the fireplace to chase away the chilliness in the cabin.

She got comfortable on the love seat and Buddy joined her there, his furry body warming her feet.

She grabbed the bag of candy she'd bought for trick-or-treaters a couple of days before...trick-or-treaters who had never come, and she unwrapped one of the miniature chocolate bars.

As she popped it into her mouth she stared into the crackling, blazing fire and for the first time in a very long time a sense of happiness swept through her.

It had been a great night as Spirit had reached a new milestone in her training. Seeing the horse being led peacefully around the corral by Mac had been not just amazing but also heartwarming. Thankfully, the frightened, abused horse was healing both physically and mentally.

When she'd first gotten the terrified horse, she'd never thought this day would come. But she hadn't counted on Mac's expertise and the magic of his music.

She couldn't help smiling as she thought of the man who had not only earned Spirit's trust but her own, as well. She'd been so happy tonight as she'd danced with him around the corral. She'd really wanted to invite him in to celebrate in a more intimate way and that was exactly why she hadn't.

There was no question she was getting too close and far too comfortable with him. And worse, she knew he was developing real, deep emotions where she was concerned. In fact, she was pretty sure he was in love with her. He wore it all over his handsome, rugged face whenever they were together. She felt it in his every touch.

And even worse than that was the fact that she was in love with him. She didn't know specifically when it had happened. But it was real and raw inside her and she definitely didn't want it. She refused to allow it.

They had spent the last month and a half talking…learning each other from the inside out. She knew what his favorite food was and the things that made him angry. They'd had deep conversations and they'd had fun ones. They'd talked about politics and world news and they'd shared their moral views and values with each other.

She couldn't imagine loving another man as much as she loved Mac. However, even if her intentions weren't to kill a man, she still wouldn't want a real, long-term relationship with Mac. She was too broken and he deserved so much better than her.

Even though it had been a wonderful evening, her thoughts about Mac depressed her. Her thoughts about herself depressed her.

She'd been invited to several Halloween parties. Zeke had called to invite her to a party at the Humes ranch, but she'd declined to go. Sissy had also invited her to a costume party at her house, but Marisa had said no.

She hadn't wanted to go out and socialize with

anyone. She didn't want to give Zeke the idea that she was open to a relationship with him. She also had no plans to pursue any further friendship with Sissy. The two old friends were in different places in their lives and they would never be able to relate to where Marisa was in hers.

Once she acted out her deepest fantasy of murder or homicide or whatever it was going to be deemed, she would once again be a circus spectacle among everyone in town. She didn't want to build any relationships just for them to fall apart.

She didn't even want to think about how her future actions would affect her mother. She hated that once again she would let Rose down, but Rose was good at distancing herself from Marisa and the things that had happened in Marisa's life. Rose was a survivor, and ultimately she would be just fine.

Marisa had spent Halloween alone, doing exactly what she was doing right now. She'd built a fire and made some hot chocolate and watched a little television.

She now remained on the love seat until it was time to go to bed. Tomorrow was once again Mac's day off, so he'd be arriving around ten in the morning to work with Spirit. She hated herself for eagerly anticipating his presence.

She knew she'd been pushing and pulling at Mac. One minute she was pulling him close and the next minute she was attempting to shove him away. Through it all she felt his steady support and love for her.

Sick of her own thoughts, she decided to call it a night. As she finally pulled herself up off the love seat, her phone rang. She froze and stared at the instrument on the end table next to her.

Her heartbeat accelerated. Her mouth dried up.

It rang a second time and she picked it up. ANONYMOUS CALLER, the identification said. It was him. She knew it in her very heart and soul. Evil seemed to emanate from the cell phone itself.

On the third ring she finally answered.

"Hello, Marisa," a deep, obviously altered yet frighteningly familiar voice said.

Just as she suspected, just as she'd dreaded and yet anticipated, it was *him.*

"What do you want?" she asked, grateful that her voice betrayed none of the icy fear that shot through her and chilled her to her very bones.

"You know what I want," he replied. "Marisa, I want you again. I told you I'd come back for you."

"Then come and get me, you twisted creep."

He laughed, and the familiar, high-pitched and ghastly sound sent new shivers up her spine. "Oh, you sound so brave. You're exciting me already."

"You are sick," she retorted.

He laughed once again. "I'm sick with want-ing you again. I've been watching you eating in the café and walking down the streets with your nose up in the air. I can't wait to see you crawling naked across the floor in the dark again."

The idea of him watching her…stalking her made her sick. Her stomach twisted as the horrible memories of her time with him rushed through her. She hated the chilling fright that swept through her. "Come and get me," she repeated, trying to sound strong and in control.

"Oh, trust me, I will. But all in due time," he finally said. "I promise you won't see me coming, Marisa. I'm going to have you again in my lair. It's just a matter of time."

He hung up before she could say anything else. Her fingers trembled as she pushed End on the call. Even though she'd tried to sound strong and ready for him to come at her again, the truth was she would be a fool not to be more than a little afraid.

And she was.

So the game had officially begun. She knew exactly what she needed to do next. She checked beneath her cushions and on all the weapons she had taped up beneath tables and then she went into her bedroom.

She opened the top drawer in her nightstand where she kept not only the condoms she had bought to use with Mac, but her gun and night vision goggles, as well.

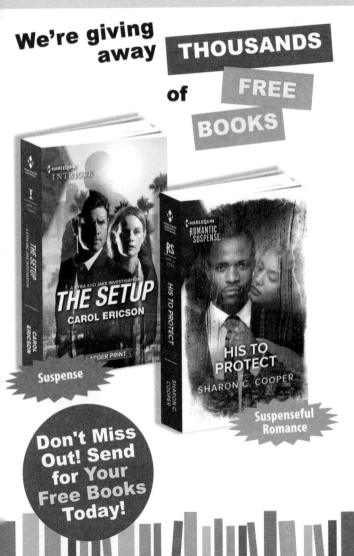

Get up to 4
FREE FABULOUS BOOKS
You Love!

To thank you for being a loyal reader we'd like to send you up to 4 FREE BOOKS, absolutely free.

Just write "YES" on the Loyal Reader Voucher and we'll send you up to 4 Free Books and Free Mystery Gifts, altogether worth over $20, as a way of saying thank you for being a loyal reader.

Try **Harlequin® Romantic Suspense** books featuring heart-racing page-turners with unexpected plot twists and irresistible chemistry that will keep you guessing to the very end.

Try **Harlequin Intrigue® Larger-Print** books featuring action-packed stories that will keep you on the edge of your seat. Solve the crime and deliver justice at all costs.

Or **TRY BOTH!**

We are so glad you love the books as much as we do and can't wait to send you great new books.

So don't miss out, return your Loyal Reader Voucher Today!

Pam Powers

LOYAL READER
FREE BOOKS VOUCHER

YES! I Love Reading, please send me up to 4 FREE BOOKS and Free Mystery Gifts from the series I select.

Just write in "YES" on the dotted line below then return this card today and we'll send your free books & gifts asap!

➡️ YES ⬅️

Which do you prefer?

☐ **Harlequin® Romantic Suspense**
240/340 HDL GRHP

☐ **Harlequin Intrigue® Larger-Print**
199/399 HDL GRHP

☐ **BOTH**
240/340 & 199/399
HDL GRHZ

FIRST NAME

LAST NAME

ADDRESS

APT.#

CITY

STATE/PROV.

ZIP/POSTAL CODE

EMAIL ☐ Please check this box if you would like to receive newsletters and promotional emails from Harlequin Enterprises ULC and its affiliates. You can unsubscribe anytime.

HI/HRS-520-LR21

HARLEQUIN Reader Service —**Here's how it works:**

She was as mentally and physically prepared as she could be to meet again with the man who had destroyed her life. This was exactly what she'd been waiting for. She'd *wanted* him to come for her again.

However, she hadn't expected to be so afraid. Theoretically, she had believed she would face this final ordeal bravely…eagerly…and not be scared. But the stakes were so high. It was her very life on the line.

One thing was very clear. Only one of them would walk away alive from this second encounter. And she could only hope it would be her.

The night was positively endless. Sleep was as elusive as a two-headed unicorn. She'd placed her gun under her pillow. She also knew if anyone came around the cabin, Buddy would let her know.

But nothing got her to calm the nerves inside her. The phone call played over and over in her mind. She found it impossible to relax even though she knew with a fair amount of certainty he wouldn't come after her tonight.

He'd want to taunt her and make more phone calls to her. He would want to send her terrible notes to increase her fear and get her freaked out. He would want the anticipation to haunt her and to terrorize her. There was no question he got off on her fear.

At some point she must have finally fallen

asleep because she suddenly came awake. She gasped for breath as her heart beat too fast. Her gaze shot around the room. What had awakened her? What had her in a fight-or-flight state of mind right now?

Then she heard Buddy. His deep, menacing growl came from the living room. What had the dog stirred up? She reached beneath her pillow and grabbed her gun. Had she been wrong? Was he coming for her right now?

She slid from the bed, her heart pounding so hard she could hear it inside her head. Was he here right this minute? In the living room? Surely if he'd broken down the door she would have heard it. If he'd come inside the house Buddy would have already attacked him.

She held the gun tightly, drew a deep, steadying breath and then whirled out of her room.

Buddy had his nose pressed to the bottom of the door as he growled deep and loud in his throat. There was nobody in the room, so if he'd come for her, he was still outside.

Obviously Buddy must have heard something to pull him out of his bed and to the door. Whatever he heard, it was clear that he considered it a threat. Aside from his menacing growl, the fur on his haunches stood on end.

Marisa had never considered what to do in this particular situation. In her visions of him coming after her, she'd always assumed he'd be able to get into the cabin.

Despite the fear that raced through her, she leaned over Buddy and unlocked the cabin's door. Buddy stood, as if anticipating what she'd do next.

Once again she drew a deep breath and allowed a burst of adrenaline to rush through her. She mentally counted to three and then she reached out and opened the door.

The darkness of the night rushed in on her, tightening her chest, as Buddy raced outside. Her eyes quickly adjusted, and she saw what Buddy was after...two small coyotes raced toward the tree line with Buddy hot on their heels.

She swept the area with her gaze and saw no sign of any two-legged creature anywhere around. A sigh rushed out of her. It was a mixture of both relief and a touch of disappointment.

"Buddy," she yelled. "Buddy, halt!"

The dog immediately stopped the chase and then ran back to the cabin and to her side. She looked around one last time and released another deep sigh. Together, they went back inside and Marisa closed and locked the door.

"Good boy." She leaned down and patted Buddy's side and continued to praise him. The coyotes had gotten too close to the house and Buddy had reacted to them as a perceived threat. That was his job... that was what he was supposed to do.

Buddy was trained not to chase most wildlife, but Marisa doubted that he'd ever encountered a coyote before. Besides, she'd rather be overprotected than underprotected.

She led the dog back into the bedroom and she returned to bed. She tucked the gun back beneath her pillow and then once again tried to relax.

She had been back in bed only a few minutes when Buddy jumped up with her. He didn't look at her as he slunk up to the pillow next to hers. It was obvious he hoped she wouldn't see him so she wouldn't send him back to his dog bed on the floor.

Even though many of the experts would say it was bad to allow a dog to sleep in a bed, tonight she wanted him close to her. "Good night, Buddy," she said softly. He released a sigh and closed his eyes.

Her brain was working too much for sleep to come. Tonight it had been coyotes, but it could have been him. It was a grim reminder that just because the last time he had called her and written her terrorizing notes for a couple of weeks before kidnapping her, it wasn't necessary that he would follow the same pattern this time.

When morning finally came she dragged herself out of bed. She'd probably only slept a couple of hours throughout the night despite having Buddy right next to her.

By the time she drank two cups of coffee she was wide awake and ready for the day even though she dreaded what she knew she now needed to do.

Her heart hung heavy in her chest as she went about her morning routine. She'd been so wrong to selfishly allow the relationship with Mac to continue knowing what her ultimate goal was.

The phone call she'd received from her tormentor had changed everything. She now had to make choices that were going to screw everything up. Without question this would be one of the most difficult days of her life.

Normally about fifteen minutes before Mac was expected to arrive, she'd go out with Buddy and set up the chairs. She'd be outside waiting for him. Today she remained inside.

With each minute that passed, her dread increased and she started to feel slightly sick to her stomach. She was seated at her kitchen table when there was a knock on the door, at precisely ten o'clock. Buddy immediately ran to the door and barked as if to let her know somebody was there in case she hadn't heard the knock.

She got up and opened the door to find Mac with a beautiful smile curving his lips and his guitar case in his hand. "Hey," he said. "Did you forget I was coming this morning?"

"No, I didn't forget." He looked so handsome in his black jacket and with his black cowboy hat pulled low across his head. His smile was warm and the gaze of his eyes even warmer.

Unexpected emotion suddenly tightened her chest and crawled up the back of her throat. Oh, this was going to be much harder than she'd expected. Her fingers gripped her door, keeping him out on the stoop. "I'm sorry, Mac, but I'm afraid we need to stop with Spirit's training."

His smile immediately transformed into a look of utter confusion. "Stop the training? Things were going so well."

"I know, but the training has to stop," she replied, sick in her very soul.

"But why, Marisa?" His gaze swept across her features as if somehow seeking an answer there. "H-have I done something wrong? Have I done something to somehow offend you?" Bewilderment now battled with concern on his face.

"Oh, no, Mac…not at all," she replied hurriedly. The last thing she'd want him to believe was that he'd done something wrong. "I…I just need to stop things right now for some personal reasons."

"Okay. So…so, what about us?"

"I really just need my alone time for now." She couldn't meet his gaze. She couldn't stand to see the hurt she knew would be in those beautiful chocolate brown eyes of his. However, she couldn't allow him to be anywhere around what was going to happen next in her life.

She didn't want Mac to be in any danger because of her. If he knew what was really happening, he would try to be a hero and he could be killed. She wouldn't have that. She absolutely had to keep him in the dark.

She also didn't want him to know what she intended to do, that this showdown was exactly what she wanted to happen, what she'd prepared herself and planned for.

"Marisa…what's going on?" he asked softly. "Look at me and tell me exactly what is happening right now."

She forced herself to meet his gaze once again. "Nothing's happening, Mac. I told you I just need some alone time right now."

"But I thought we were…"

"We were what?" She interrupted whatever he'd been about to say and tried to harden her heart against him. She had to, even though it broke her own heart. "Mac, I warned you at the beginning of all this that I wasn't looking for any kind of a relationship."

"Yes, but I thought over the past couple of weeks we'd grown beyond that." He still had more than a little bit of confusion on his features.

"Well, we haven't," she said harshly. "Just because I slept with you a couple of times and you're good in bed doesn't mean I want to have you in my life forever."

She heard his shocked, slight intake of breath. She positively hated herself for what she was doing to him. This was all her fault. She should have never allowed things to go as far as they had with him. She'd been weak where he was concerned and now he was paying the price for her own mistake.

"Mac, please just leave it alone. Please just leave me alone."

"Are you sure that's what you want?"

"I'm positive," she replied with as much firmness as she could muster.

He stared at her for several long moments and then gave a curt nod of his head. "If that's what you really want."

"It is," she replied. She was in agony as she watched his eyes go dark and shuttered. She knew that behind those shutters was a wealth of pain... pain she had put there.

"What about Spirit?" he asked. "She still needs further work."

"I'll take care of it," she replied briskly. All she wanted now was for him to go away so she wouldn't have to see the hurt in his eyes, so that she wouldn't weaken and tell him she wanted... she needed him after all. Tears burned at her eyes and she definitely didn't want him to see her cry.

She looked down but felt his gaze on her for another minute. "Okay, then," he finally said. "Then I guess I'll just see you around." He took a step back from the door. "Marisa, call me if you need anything…anything at all."

She nodded, her emotion crawling up her throat and choking off any other words she might have said.

Still he remained, as if intentionally torturing her with his continued presence. "About Spirit… it's an important time in her training. I'd hate to see her go backward. Are you going to hire somebody else to continue to work with her?"

"To be honest, I haven't thought about that yet, but you can believe I'll make whatever decision I need to in the best interest of Spirit. And now I'll just say goodbye, Mac."

She didn't wait for him to reply. She couldn't stand to listen to anything else he might say. Even the sound of his beautiful, deep voice now broke her heart.

She closed her door and locked it and then leaned weakly against it as tears pressed hot at her eyes. She placed a hand over her mouth to keep any sobs from escaping.

She only cried in her nightmares but she now found herself crying over the loss of Mac. The tears chased down her cheeks as her knees weakened and a deep sob managed to escape.

Only in her dreams had she imagined what might have been between them. If only she hadn't been ruined. If only she hadn't put herself on a mission of death.

However, she had, and she had definitely messed things up between them now. Once he got over her sudden withdrawal from him, he'd probably hate her.

Dammit, she'd known all along that she would not have a future with the cowboy who made her feel safe and had brought her laughter back, who'd comforted her and made her feel desired.

For the last couple of weeks she'd been living in a fantasy world. She'd been living her life with Mac as if she had a right to be happy, as if they really had a future together.

It was all over now. She swiped at the tears from her cheeks and half fell onto the love seat. At least he wouldn't get drawn into the next chapter of her life, a chapter where somebody was going to die.

While her plan was to kill the man who had destroyed her life, the person who had stolen her peace and ability to seek happiness, she was aware that if it all went wrong, then she would be the one who died.

The single phone call she had received the night before had made it necessary to cut Mac out of her life. It was probably a good thing anyway.

After all, the truth of the matter was she really was a woman with only hatred and vengeance in her heart... She really was a woman with no future.

Chapter 8

Mac was completely shell-shocked. As he drove away from Marisa's cabin he wondered what in the heck had just happened. The woman he'd just spoken to wasn't the same woman he had left the night before.

When he reached the place where he had to turn to go back into Bitterroot and the Holiday ranch, he pulled over and parked. He needed time to think. He couldn't believe this was the end of him working with Spirit. He definitely didn't want to believe this was the end of his relationship with Marisa.

No matter how many times she said it he didn't

believe that he'd been nothing more to her than a good time in bed. His heart and his head told him differently.

What could have happened between last night and this morning? Last night they had left each other on a high note. What could have possibly happened to make her cut him so cleanly out of her life?

Had she heard some sort of gossip about him that was unsavory? If so, it could only be a lie. His life was about as exciting as a dog napping on a porch. No, her reaction couldn't be because of anything she could've learned about him.

So, what had happened?

He was bewildered, and there was no question that he was hurt. His heart banged in his chest in a broken rhythm of despair. He couldn't picture not having Marisa in his life. He couldn't imagine not spending time with her, or holding her or making love to her ever again.

However, as he remained parked and thinking about what had just happened between them, a little bit of anger also rose up inside him and battled with the pain.

Surely after all this time, after everything they had shared together, he deserved more than what she'd just given him? Telling him she needed to be alone was far too vague and inexplicable. She owed him real answers, and dammit, he was going to go get them.

With a sense of purpose he turned his truck around and headed back to the cabin. He was damned and determined he wasn't leaving until he got some real answers as to what was going on with her.

He roared back down the lane and pulled up in front of the cabin. As he stalked back to the front door, Spirit walked toward the corral railing as if to greet him.

Under any other circumstances Mac would have greeted the horse with affection, but he wasn't here now to bond with the animal or sweet-talk anyone. He wanted answers from the horse's beautiful owner, and he didn't intend to go away until he got them.

As he knocked on the door for the second time, his heart banged in his chest. Buddy barked from inside and then the door cracked open a bit.

Her eyes widened at the sight of him. "Mac," she said in obvious surprise. "Wh-what are you doing back here? I thought I made myself very clear to you."

"You didn't make anything clear to me. I'm not satisfied with the way we just left things. Marisa. You owe me some real answers as to why you're all of a sudden choosing to shove me not just out of Spirit's training but out of your life. And I'll warn you right now, I'm not leaving without those answers."

She closed her eyes for a long moment and released a deep sigh. She must have recognized the determination in his voice. She opened her eyes and paused for another long beat, and then finally opened the door to allow him entry.

Buddy greeted him immediately, nudging his hand for some loving. Mac complied, scratching him on the head and then stroking down his furry side.

"Have a seat," Marisa said and gestured him toward the love seat. She sank down on the chair opposite him.

Now that Mac really looked at her, it appeared she had been crying. Her eyes were red and slightly swollen. What had she been weeping about? If sending him away had made her sad enough to cry, then why had she done it in the first place? She crossed her arms in front of her defensively. Her eyes were dark and shuttered against him.

"What's really going on, Marisa?" he asked.

"What makes you think it's anything other than I just want to be alone right now?"

He leaned forward. "Because I think you've enjoyed having me in your life, not just as your horse trainer but also as a friend and lover. We haven't fought, we haven't had any kind of a disagreement that would warrant you just up and sending me away, so I want a real, honest answer as to what is going on with you right now."

"I've told you I don't want a relationship and I...I don't want you to get hurt."

It was too late. He'd known he was headed for heartache with her and still he'd continued to see her. "Marisa, I'm in charge of my own heart and you don't have to be, so that's an argument that has no standing. If I get hurt, then it's my choice. But the last thing I want is just to be unceremoniously dumped out of your life without knowing why it's happening."

He leaned back once again. "If you're tired of my company, then tell me that, but don't give me that line about you needing to be alone. I deserve more than that."

"Please, Mac. Why can't you just let it go?"

"Because I can't. Because this is too important to me," he replied fervently. "Because you're too important to me."

She frowned. "Are you always so stubborn?"

"Only about things that matter, and you definitely, really matter to me, Marisa."

She looked down, but not before he saw a glint of tears in her eyes. "Marisa, why are you crying? Please just talk to me. We've always been honest with each other. Just tell me the real reason you sent me away earlier."

She finally looked back up at him. "He called me last night." The words seemed to explode out of her. "He's coming for me again and I don't want you anywhere around me. I couldn't live with myself if you got hurt."

Mac stared at her in stunned surprise as his mind worked frantically to take in what she'd just told him. The perp had called her? He'd told her he was coming after her again?

"Are you crazy? If he told you he's coming after you again then the last thing you should do is send me away. If he called you, then you need to contact Dillon immediately and report it if you haven't already done so."

"I haven't contacted him because it was an anonymous call. So there's really nothing Dillon can do about it," she countered.

"That may or may not be the case, but he still needs to know that this case is active once again. If he's going to catch this creep then he needs to know everything that's going on," Mac said firmly. "Let me call him for you, Marisa."

She hesitated a long moment and then finally nodded. "Okay, fine, if you want to call him, then go ahead."

Mac dug his cell phone out of his pocket and dialed Dillon's number. "Dillon, can you come out to Marisa's cabin as soon as possible?"

"Sure, what's up?" Dillon asked.

"There's been a development in Marisa's case," Mac said.

"Give me fifteen minutes and I'll be out there," Dillon replied.

"Thanks, Dillon." Mac ended the call and looked back at Marisa. "Talking to Dillon is just the first thing you need to do," he said.

He stood and began to pace the floor in front of her. "Now that you got this phone call why don't you move into an apartment downtown? Or move in with your mother? Hell, pack a few bags and tonight you and Buddy can move into my little room at the Holiday ranch for the time being. At least I know you'll be safe there."

She frowned at him. "That's why I didn't want you to know what was going on...because I knew one of the first things you would try to do was force me out of here. I'm not leaving my home." She lifted her chin in obvious defiance. "I'm not going to allow you to move me out of here or this creep to chase me out."

"Then let me move in here with you," Mac countered.

She sighed in frustration. "This is exactly why I sent you away earlier today. Don't you get it? I don't want you in the middle of this, Mac. This isn't your fight."

"But it *is* my fight," he protested. "I care about you, Marisa, and that makes it my fight."

"If you really care about me, then you'll let me do this by myself. You'll let me handle this my way," she retorted. "Mac, I'm telling you right now, you aren't moving in here. I have Buddy and I have a gun. I'll be just fine alone, right here."

Mac returned to the love seat and sank back down, frustrated with what she was telling him. The very last thing he wanted was for her to be living out here by herself, knowing that a dangerous stalker was after her.

The man who had given her sixty days of hell had called to tell her he was coming back for her. How could she not be terrified and running any place where she would be safer than in this isolated cabin, all by herself? And how could he walk away and leave her, not knowing what might happen to her when he was gone? How could she even expect that of him?

They fell quiet as they waited for Dillon to arrive. She remained with her arms crossed and her eyes darkly shuttered, making it impossible for him to read what she might be thinking. He wanted to pull her up out of her chair and shake some sense into her. Of course he would never really do that, but he wanted her to rethink everything she might've planned to do right now.

Mac had a feeling she was not only angry with him for sticking his nose in her business, but also with herself for telling him about the phone call in the first place. Thank goodness she had. Whether she knew it or not, she desperately needed help. There was no way Mac wanted her facing the monster all on her own.

Finally Dillon arrived. When he knocked, Buddy went to the door and barked and growled. Marisa got out of the chair and placed her hand on Buddy's head. "Friend," she said to the dog and then opened the door to allow the police chief inside.

"Dillon." Mac stood and shook the other man's hand. "Thanks for coming out so quickly."

"No problem," Dillon replied.

"Please, have a seat." Marisa gestured him to the chair and then she and Mac sat on the love seat. Despite her pleasant tone with Dillon, Mac could feel the tense energy wafting from her.

"You didn't give me any details when you called. You definitely piqued my curiosity by telling me the case was active again. What's happened and why exactly am I here?" Dillon asked. He looked at Mac and then at Marisa.

"I got a phone call last night from the man who kidnapped me almost two years ago," Marisa said.

Dillon's dark brows rose in obvious surprise and then he pulled a notebook and pen from his wallet. "You're sure it was him?"

"Positive," Marisa replied firmly. "Although the call came in as an anonymous one."

"He's probably using a burner phone. What did he say to you?" Dillon leaned forward.

"He basically told me he's coming for me again." For the first time Mac heard a faint whisper of fear in her voice. Good, he thought. As far as he was concerned she was being far too cavalier about the whole thing and she needed to be more afraid. She needed to be scared to death.

"Obviously you didn't recognize the voice," Dillon said.

She shook her head. "No, it was digitally altered like it was the last time when I was with him."

"Was anything about his speech familiar in cadence or the specific words he chose?" Dillon asked. "Did any of those things remind you of somebody you know?"

"No," she replied.

"What about background noise? Did you hear anything that might give us a clue as to his whereabouts or identity?"

Marisa frowned. "No, I don't think there was any background noise at all."

"Did he give you a timetable? When is he planning on coming after you again?" Dillon appeared as worried as Mac felt.

"No, but if it goes like the last time then he'll call me and send me nasty notes for about two weeks or so and then he'll be ready to take me."

Marisa wrapped her arms around herself once again.

"But we can't rely on the timetable of this creep," Mac said. "Just because that's what he did in the past doesn't mean he'll do that this time. He could act at any moment." Mac sighed in frustration. "And why did he become fixated on Marisa in the first place?"

"Stalkers are strange animals," Dillon said, the frown on his face deepening. "They stalk women for a variety of reasons and it's often hard for normal people to understand."

He looked back at Marisa. "From what you told us during the investigation last time, he seemed angry with you. He wanted to punish you for some reason."

"And I can't think of anything I've done that would intentionally hurt anyone," she replied.

"Since being back in Bitterroot have you thought of any suspects?"

"Actually I have," she replied after a moment of hesitation. Mac looked at her in surprise. "I could be completely wrong, but I've wondered if Zeke Osmond or Brendon Timber might possibly be him."

"What makes you think it might be one of those men?" Dillon asked.

Mac felt the tension radiating from her. He would have loved to throw his arm around her shoulder and pull her close against him, but he had no idea if she would welcome that comfort, especially right now.

"I know it sounds kind of crazy, but I've been thinking about anyone who I might have wronged in my past. The only thing I can think of is that when I was in high school I knew Zeke and Brendon both had crushes on me, but I never went out with either of them. Since I've been back here both of them have repeatedly asked me out." She paused and drew a deep breath. "But it seems really crazy to believe that one of them held a grudge against me for almost ten years and then decided to kidnap me."

"Brendon appears to be a decent man, but nothing would surprise me when it comes to Zeke," Mac said darkly. Mac's hands fisted as he thought of what he'd like to do to the man who had kidnapped and tortured Marisa. He was surprised that Marisa hadn't told him that both of those men had asked her out a number of times.

"Still, the timetable does seem a bit odd. To believe that somebody who was rejected in high school waited ten years for revenge," he said.

"Not necessarily," Dillon replied. "That's the thing with stalkers. Some triggering event possibly occurred in his life that reminded him of that long-ago rejection and suddenly it grew bigger and more difficult to ignore."

"So, what's the game plan now?" Mac asked. "She insists she's going to stay out here all alone." Mac was hoping for a second voice of reason that might make her rethink that plan.

"Marisa, I would certainly recommend that you think about moving in with friends or with your mother for a couple of weeks while we continue to investigate, but I can't make that decision for you," Dillon said. He stood. "Is there any other information you have for me?"

Marisa shook her head. "That's all I've got. I know you can't do anything about the phone call, but Mac insisted I tell you about it."

"As you should have," Dillon asserted. "Marisa, I need to know anything and everything that goes on with you. If you get more phone calls, let me know. If you get letters or notes, call me and I'll come to collect them." His eyes narrowed. "We didn't catch this creep before, but I'm damned and determined to catch him before he acts against you again."

"Thank you for coming out, Dillon," she said as she got up to walk him to the door.

"I'll walk you out," Mac said to Dillon.

The two men walked out into the bright sunshine and headed for Dillon's official vehicle. "I'm worried sick about this, Dillon. She refuses to leave the cabin. I offered to move in with her to help keep her safe, but she rejected that idea, too. She thinks she can handle this all on her own."

"I hear your pain but, Mac, you and I both know we can't force her to do anything. I wish I had extra men who could do guard duty on her, but I don't. Unfortunately, the police department is ridiculously understaffed right now."

"I understand," Mac said. He knew that several officers had quit the department and moved to bigger cities to continue their careers in law enforcement. He just wished things were different and Dillon could provide constant security.

"What I intend to do right now is have a long chat with both Brendon and Zeke. I need to check into their work schedules and find out if either of them had a place to hide Marisa the last time she was in captivity. She was held someplace for sixty days and it's possible one of them has property I don't know about. Neither of them was even on the radar when we investigated the first time, so I've got my work cut out for me in doing a deep dive into both of them."

"They are definitely on my radar now," Mac half growled.

"You leave this all to me, Mac. Don't you go off half-cocked and ruin my investigation," Dillon warned.

Mac stuck his hands in his pockets. "You know

I won't do that. I'm just so damned worried about Marisa."

"And that makes two of us. Let's hope she's right and he won't act for at least another two weeks." Dillon opened his car door. "That gives me fourteen days or so to figure out who the stalker is, and on that note, I'd better get out of here and get to work."

Mac watched the lawman drive off, a sense of real urgency filling him. It was as if there was a time bomb beneath Marisa and she was purposely ignoring it.

He turned and headed back to the cabin, hoping he'd be able to talk some sense into her.

Mac packed up several blankets and a large thermos of hot coffee into the back of his pickup. It was dusk, and night would be here soon. He wanted to be in place when the darkness came.

Trying to talk to Marisa earlier in the day after Dillon had left had been like trying to converse with a rock. Much to his frustration, she'd reiterated her desire to remain alone in the cabin, although she did finally agree to let him continue with Spirit's training. That had felt like a hollow victory when he was so worried about her safety.

She'd told Mac she'd decided to put all her trust in Dillon catching the perp before he acted again. Mac didn't have that kind of trust.

He believed Dillon Bowie was a great chief of police and a top-notch investigator, but Dillon couldn't solve a crime if there weren't any clues. So far, all he had was an anonymous phone call and the names of two men who might or might not be the perp, and that certainly wasn't enough to lead to an arrest that would keep Marisa safe.

Since there was no way Dillon could provide 24/7 security, Mac had decided to be secret service for Marisa. In fact he was going to be so secret he hoped she wouldn't even know he was there.

He'd spoken to Cassie and had gotten the next two weeks off work. He had plenty of vacation time accrued, so she hadn't had a problem with him taking the time off.

He had a tentative plan in theory in his head to try to keep Marisa safe, but he had no idea how the plan would work in reality. It was going to be a bit complicated but he believed it was doable.

All he knew for certain was that there was no way he was going to leave Marisa to her own devices when it came to her protection against some madman who wanted to kidnap her once again.

He had to do whatever he could to help keep her safe, if nothing else but for his own sanity. There was no way he could just go about his own business knowing she was so vulnerable. Besides, what she didn't know wouldn't hurt her.

Grabbing a good flashlight and making sure his gun belt held his revolver around his hips, he got into his truck and headed out.

It was a cool night with thick clouds chasing across the moon. There was some rain expected to move in later in the night. Mac didn't care if the forecast was for a monsoon or a blizzard; he intended to be where he could spring into action should danger come anywhere near Marisa.

His mind worked overtime as he drove from the Holiday ranch to the Lindale place. He'd somehow hoped he would have heard from Dillon after he'd spoken to Zeke and Brendon. He knew Dillon would have called him if anything had broken in the case. The silence from the lawman made it obvious nothing had happened.

Mac was praying for a miracle… He desperately wished Dillon would find and arrest the guilty party within the next couple of days…long before this creep had an opportunity to do anything.

He turned into the drive of the Lindale place and drove on down the dirt road to the cattle gate. Once he was through that he saw a thick copse of trees that was fairly close to the cabin.

He parked the truck in the thick of the trees where it was hidden from view and pulled everything he'd brought with him out of the bed. In all the time he'd spent with Marisa, he'd never seen her move aside her window coverings to peer outside. He hoped she wouldn't do so now.

There was just a last gasp of light left in the day as he approached the corral. Spirit stood in the middle of the wooden enclosure. "Hey, pretty girl," he said softly. "Hey, sweet baby."

He hoped Spirit wouldn't mind sharing her shelter for the next fourteen days and nights. He walked into the shed and flipped on his flashlight to get his bearings.

There was just enough space on the side of the horse stall for him to make a small bed with some of the extra sweet-smelling hay in the bottom of the stall. He pulled it out and made himself a small nest.

Once he was settled in with his blankets and coffee, he turned off the flashlight. Darkness descended and Mac sat and poured himself a cup of the hot brew from the thermos.

The night was quiet except for the soft clicking and whirring of night insects. If anyone attempted to approach the cabin, Mac would be able to hear him coming. He would coordinate his schedule so Marisa wouldn't know he was out here and on guard for her. She'd insisted she didn't want him involved in this, but as a man who loved her, he'd go to whatever lengths necessary to keep her safe from harm.

Although he knew evil could happen in the

brightness of the day, he felt in his bones that Marisa's tormentor would come in the darkness of the night. And Mac was determined to be here when that happened.

The minutes ticked by and the darkness grew deeper. A rumble of thunder sounded in the distance. He wondered if Spirit would come into the stable if it rained, or would his presence here keep her out? He hoped not. The last thing he would want was for Spirit to remain outside in the middle of a storm because of him.

Another half an hour or so passed. Lightning split the skies and lit up the interior of the small shed. Thunder boomed overhead and rain began to pitter-patter on the roof. He sensed Spirit just outside the shed. *Come on, girl*, he thought. *Be brave enough to get out of the rain.*

After several minutes the rain intensified and he heard the horse just outside the shed, sniffing the air. She finally walked into the stall.

Despite the circumstances Mac felt a new sense of contentment. Spirit knew he was here but had trusted him enough to come inside. Both his girls were safe for the night. Spirit was safe from the elements outside, and Marisa was protected with him on guard duty.

The rain fell for several hours and then finally stopped. He was grateful for the blankets and the hot coffee he'd brought as the night had grown cold.

He remained on high alert throughout the night. Just before dawn he packed up all his things and crept back to his truck. He then headed back to the Holiday ranch.

After a refreshing shower and a change of clothes, he headed around to the dining room for breakfast. He'd just filled his plate and sat at a table when Dusty joined him.

"Hey, man, Sawyer told me earlier this morning that you were on vacation," Dusty said. "So, what are you doing here? You should be on a beach somewhere."

"Ha, like I'm really the beach type," Mac replied with a laugh. "Actually, I'm on secret guard duty." Mac explained what had happened with the phone call to Marisa and the timeline they believed she was on.

"Wow, that's so messed up," Dusty said when Mac had finished explaining everything. "So, what are you planning?"

"For starters, unbeknownst to her, I'm staying in her shed every night. My gut instinct tells me this creep will come in the dark. I don't think he'll take a chance coming after her in the daytime even with her out in the middle of nowhere. But if he does… I'll be there. In fact, once I eat I'm going back to the shed."

"That's going to be a difficult schedule for you to keep," Dusty said. "You do that for a couple of days and you'll probably be half-dead."

"I know it's going to be a challenge, but if this guy's timeline holds true, then he'll come after her in the next thirteen days."

God, the idea of Marisa being in the hands of this perp again twisted his gut and stabbed his heart with daggers of pain. He couldn't understand why she wasn't taking all precautions in the world to protect herself, but as long as she wasn't, he would.

"Mac, you know that you can count on any of us here to help you out in any way. All you have to do is ask," Dusty said.

"Thanks, Dusty. I'll keep that in mind." His heart expanded as he thought about the many times in the past the twelve "brothers" had pulled together to help one of them in need.

"I sure miss seeing some of the guys," he continued. "Especially Forest." Forest Stevens had been the other horse trainer with Mac. When bodies had been uncovered beneath an old shed on the Holiday property, Dr. Patience Forbes, a forensic anthropologist, had been brought in to try to identify the skeletal remains. Forest and the petite red-haired spitfire had fallen hard for each other.

When she'd left to go back to her home in Oklahoma City, Forest had gone with her. While he'd stayed in touch with some of the men with occasional phone calls, they were all so busy with their own lives that keeping in touch with everyone who had left the ranch was hit-and-miss.

"It would be awesome if we could arrange some kind of reunion with everyone," Dusty now said.

"That would be great, but right now all I have on my mind is keeping Marisa safe," Mac replied.

"I certainly understand that," Dusty said. "It's just kind of strange that Marisa wants to stay in the cabin knowing this guy is coming for her again."

"Yeah, I don't get it," Mac replied.

"Let's just hope Dillon can arrest the creep before he gets a chance to even get close to Marisa."

"That's definitely my hope, too," Mac said.

He ate quickly and then went back to the kitchen where Cookie sat at a small table with a cup of coffee before him.

He looked at Mac and scowled. "What are you doing in my kitchen?"

Mac had no idea how a balding older man whom he'd grown up with could intimidate him so much, but Cookie managed to intimidate all the cowboys he fed.

"I…I wonder if you would mind if I make myself a couple of sandwiches? I won't be here for lunch or dinner and I need some food to take with me."

Cookie rose from his chair. "You aren't doing anything in my kitchen. Sit and I'll take care of things." He pointed Mac to the chair he had just vacated.

Mac sat and watched as Cookie went to a cabinet and pulled out a medium-sized cooler. Within minutes the cook had packed two thick sandwiches, a container of potato salad and another of fresh fruit. He added three bottles of water and a chunk of chocolate cake big enough for three men. Silverware and napkins topped it all off.

"Cookie, have you ever considered getting remarried?" Mac asked. He knew Cookie's wife and child had died in a home fire years before he'd ever come to work for Big Cass, but he had no idea if the man had any kind of dating relationship now or not.

He lived in the foreman's cabin on the property, but Mac and the others knew nothing about Cookie's life outside of what he did in the kitchen.

"Never," Cookie replied. "I loved my wife and when she was gone I never wanted another woman in my life. I got it right the first time with her and have never wanted or needed to try it again." He set the cooler in front of Mac. "So, is this all about a woman?"

Mac nodded. "A woman in danger."

"You talking about Marisa Lindale?"

Mac looked at the old man in surprise. "How did you know that?"

Cookie offered Mac one of his rare grins. "I know a lot more about all you boys than you think."

"That's a little bit scary," Mac said wryly.

"You just keep yourself safe," Cookie said gruffly. "Now, you got what you came for, so get out of my kitchen."

"Thanks, Cookie." Mac flashed him a grin, grabbed the cooler and then headed out of the dining area. He walked quickly to the vehicle shed and got back into his pickup.

His plan was to hide in the shed until after dinnertime and then he'd officially arrive for Spirit's training. The only thing that really worried him was Buddy. The dog might give away his hiding place. Worse, the dog might attack him if he found Mac alone in the shed.

Exhaustion tugged at him. He yawned and realized the night of no sleep was already catching up with him. He figured he could catnap some during the day and prepare himself for another night of no sleep.

He knew that if Marisa caught him out here, she'd be angry with him, and that was something he just didn't understand. He shoved these thoughts out of his head as he parked beneath the trees in the same place he had parked the night before.

He got out of the truck, straightened his gun belt, and then grabbed the cooler and blankets and took off walking. Hopefully, by this time of the morning Buddy had already been outside to do his business and Marisa wouldn't suddenly emerge from the cabin.

As he walked, he kept to the tree lines as long as possible. Thankfully, the rain that had fallen through the night was gone, leaving beautiful blue skies overhead. The bright sunshine had already dried out most of the rain.

Spirit was in the corral. She nickered a greeting as Mac approached. Mac returned to his little nest in the shed and settled in for a long day.

Even though he intended to nap, he knew he wouldn't sleep so deeply that he wouldn't hear anyone approaching the cabin. A lot of trees had shed their leaves, creating a floor of crunchy bedding that would alert him if anyone came close.

After several minutes his eyes drifted closed and he fell into a light sleep. Buddy's bark awoke him. He sat up, every muscle tense.

A moment later Buddy came barreling into the shed. Instead of growling or attacking, the dog licked the side of Mac's face. "Hey, Buddy," Mac petted him and then gave him a little push. "Go do your business, Buddy. Go on." Buddy obviously didn't see Mac as any kind of a threat.

The dog plopped down beside him and rolled over on his back. Mac scratched his belly for a moment and then tried to push him away once again. The last thing he wanted was for Marisa to come and look for her dog and find Mac hiding out in here.

A few minutes later he heard the cabin door open. "Buddy?" Marisa yelled.

Thankfully, the dog jumped up and ran out of the shed. Mac breathed a sigh of relief. At least he knew now that Buddy wasn't going to be a problem.

He managed to catnap through the afternoon and at one point ate one of the sandwiches and some of the fruit Cookie had prepared for him.

At five o'clock he snuck back to his truck and at five thirty he drove to the cabin and parked in front. He couldn't help the way his heart beat in anticipation of seeing her again. He couldn't help that he'd fallen hopelessly in love with her.

All he could hope for now was that he could keep her alive and the man who filled her eyes with that haunted look…the bastard who had stolen sixty days of her life would be caught and put into jail for the rest of his life.

The alternative to that was too horrible to even

contemplate. If something happened to her on his watch, it wouldn't just hurt him…it would absolutely destroy him.

Chapter 9

Marisa sat next to Mac as he played his guitar. Normally the music would soothe not only Spirit but her, as well. But tonight she refused to let the music or the man in.

She'd caught up on her sleepless night by napping off and on during the day. However, she didn't feel rested. Rather, she felt restless and on edge.

For the first time since Mac had been coming to work with Spirit, she worked hard to stay completely disconnected from him. She had to keep her emotions in check, where he was concerned.

She would have preferred he not be here at all,

but ultimately she had caved, for Spirit's sake. But there would be no more invites into the cabin and no more sleepovers with him. She had to remain strong and keep him out of her heart. She had to stay focused on her one goal, the thing that had driven her life for the past sixteen months.

Besides, if Mac could look into her heart and soul and see the darkness, the rage and the hatred that lived there, he wouldn't want anything to do with her anymore.

The music stopped and he set the guitar aside. "You're very quiet tonight," he said. She felt his gaze on her even though she stared straight ahead. "Are you afraid, Marisa?" His soft voice broke the sudden silence.

She finally turned to look at him. "Not at all. I told you yesterday that with my gun and Buddy I feel completely safe here. Hopefully, Dillon is doing his job and he'll catch the man before he can come after me again."

Mac frowned. "Dillon can't catch the bad guy if he doesn't have any clues."

"I gave him two names of potential suspects yesterday."

"Do you really believe Zeke or Brendon is the person who took you before?"

She released a deep sigh. "I can't be sure, Mac. But they were the only two off the top of my head that I could think of who might have an issue with me, even though those issues occurred years ago."

"I just can't believe somebody would wait ten years to stalk you for things that did or didn't happen in high school," he said.

"I really don't want to talk about any of this right now. I told you I'm leaving it all up to Dillon. That's all I have to say on the matter."

She could tell her answer frustrated him, but she couldn't do anything about that. He shouldn't even be here now.

"Let's go inside the corral and do some work with Spirit," he said.

She nodded and rose from the chair. For the next hour, under Mac's instructions, she led Spirit around the corral in an effort to continue to bond with the horse.

Although there were times when Spirit offered some resistance, for the most part the progress they'd made with her filled Marisa with joy.

"She's going to be a really good horse," she said to Mac once they were finished working for the night.

"I think she's going to be a great horse," Mac replied as they walked back toward their chairs.

"Mac…could I ask you a really important question?"

"Of course," he replied instantly, as she knew he would.

"If…if anything happens to me will you take Spirit and Buddy with you and keep them on the Holiday ranch?" She stopped walking to gaze at him once again. His face blanched.

A wealth of emotion suddenly rose up inside her, and before he could say anything, she reached out and gripped his forearm tightly. "Promise me, Mac. This is so important to me. Please…promise me you'll take care of them and love them if I'm not around."

His eyes flashed darkly. "Marisa, don't ask me that… Don't even think like that."

"Just promise me, Mac." Even though she believed herself ready for the perpetrator, there was always the risk that she would lose the fight and he'd capture her once again and this time forever. If that happened she needed to know that her beloved horse and dog would be taken care of.

His gaze held hers for several long moments. "Okay, I promise, but I wish you would accept my help in keeping you safe."

"I'm fine the way things are." She released her grip from his arm, relieved that he had agreed.

"And yet you're making contingency plans in case you get kidnapped again." His frustration was rife in his voice. "Does that make any sense to you? Do you have some sort of a death wish?"

She broke eye contact with him and folded up her chair. "Of course not," she scoffed.

"Then why won't you let me help you?"

"I don't need your help. And I told you I don't want to talk about any of this anymore. I'm tired and it's getting dark. I'm ready to call it a night."

She needed to get away from Mac before she threw herself into his arms. Darkness was quickly approaching, danger was drawing near, and all she could think of was how wonderful it would be to fall asleep with his big strong arms wrapped tightly around her.

"I'll take care of the chairs," he said. He folded his and then took hers from her hand. She watched as he carried them into the shed.

She kept having to remind herself that there was really no future with Mac. She might have once been good enough for a man like Mac, but that was before another man had broken her soul into a million pieces.

An hour later she sat at the kitchen table with a baked chicken breast and steamed broccoli before her. She really wasn't hungry, but she knew she had to eat. When the showdown happened she had to be on top of her game.

Do you have some sort of a death wish?

Mac's question played and replayed in her mind. Of course she didn't *want* to wind up dead, but she'd rather be dead than in the hands of her madman again. She would rather be dead than endure a single hour of darkness with that creep again. She didn't have a death wish, but she definitely wished death on another.

The reason why she'd spent so many months training and learning self-defense was so she wouldn't be a captive again. She intended to kill the man who came after her, but she couldn't foresee what might happen after that.

She couldn't see Mac loving her after that. In truth she didn't really think Mac was in love with her now. Oh, he might think he was, but she believed much of her allure to him was that she was a "new," rather mysterious woman in town.

He'd fallen in love with her horse and somehow those feelings had spilled onto her, but she hadn't shown him who the real Marisa was. And once he knew who she really was, he'd realize he didn't...he couldn't love her.

It was five days later that her mother made one of her rare calls to Marisa, letting her know there was mail for her at the house.

It was just after noon when Marisa took off walking from the cabin toward the big house, with a gun at her waist, a long, sharp knife tucked into her boots, and Buddy at her side.

There had been no other phone calls from *him* but she could already guess what kind of mail had been delivered to her. It could only be a note from *him*. The timing was right for a threatening note.

For the past five days, she'd continued to attempt to keep herself emotionally distant from Mac each time he came to work with Spirit. However, it had been very difficult.

There had been moments when she'd wanted to reach up and brush back a strand of his shaggy hair from his eyes, times when she'd just felt like falling into his arms, seeing so much caring in his eyes.

Her emotions where he was concerned were so close to the surface. She wanted to laugh with him again, and dance around the corral. She wanted his naked body next to hers, loving her like she'd never been loved before. Yet, she wanted to protect him at all costs.

She wanted all the things she knew she couldn't have, but it was important to maintain her emotional distance from Mac. It was the only way she knew to get through what was about to come.

As she and Buddy walked on toward the big house, she pulled her coat up around her neck. A cold front had moved through overnight. Thankfully, it was only supposed to hang around for a couple of days before milder temperatures returned.

Thanksgiving was a little over two weeks away. Mac had told her how wonderful the holiday feast was on the ranch and had invited her to come as his guest. She'd declined the invitation. In two weeks she could be dead.

Even without everything happening in her life, she wouldn't have gone with him to enjoy the holiday. She'd initially distanced herself from Mac because of what was about to happen. She now realized she would have needed to stay away from him in any case. She would never be good enough for a man like Mac and it was just as well that once Spirit's training was over he'd probably find some other woman to love.

Once she got to her mother's house, she knocked on the back door, then opened it and stepped into the huge family room with Buddy. This room was staged to appear warm and inviting, but there had never been any real family time spent there, especially after her father's death.

"Mother?" she yelled. "I'm here."

"I'm in the dining room," her mother's voice called out.

Marisa walked into the formal dining room where her mother sat at the head of a long table. "I was just having some lunch. Would you like Debra to fix you a plate?" Debra Hightower had worked as cook and housekeeper for the family for years.

Rose Lindale was still a very beautiful woman. Her long dark hair was twisted into a neat bun at the nape of her neck and the royal blue blouse she wore emphasized the bright blue of her eyes.

"No, thanks, I already ate," Marisa replied.

Rose frowned. "You know I don't like it when you bring that animal inside the house."

"He's clean and he's well-behaved. Besides, I didn't plan on staying. I know how busy you are these days with the campaign and the upcoming election."

Rose smiled like a cat with a tasty canary. "Word on the street is I'm going to win by a landslide."

"I'm not surprised. You've always gotten what you've gone after."

For the next few minutes Rose talked about her plans as mayor for the small town. Marisa wished her mother would get as animated when she spoke of her daughter as she did about her ambitions.

"I still can't believe you cut off all your beautiful hair," Rose said and shook her head. "And I really wish you'd dress up a little more when you went into town."

It was obvious one of her mother's cronies had been whispering in her ear about Marisa. It was nothing new and Marisa had learned long ago just to ignore it. "I'm always presentable when I go into town," she replied.

Their conversations almost always ended with Rose criticizing her and that meant it was time for Marisa to make her exit. "You said you had some mail for me?"

"Yes, a letter came for you. I put it on the top of the entertainment center in the family room."

"Then I'll just get it and head back to the cabin," Marisa said.

Minutes later she was walking quickly back toward the cabin, the piece of mail burning in her hand. There had been no postage stamp on it, indicating that somebody had just put it in Rose's mailbox. It was addressed to Marisa. Her name and the address were handwritten in bold, black ink.

Even though the letter was forefront in her mind, thoughts of her mother also lingered in her head. Rose had never asked her daughter any details about what had happened to her in those sixty days of captivity. She had never held Marisa in her arms and offered her solace.

Other than partially blaming Marisa for what had happened to her, Rose preferred to pretend the whole thing had never occurred. Marisa was aware that Rose believed Marisa was now nothing more than an embarrassment.

Marisa had never felt like she had her mother's love and support. Even when Marisa was a cheerleader and the town's sweetheart, her mother had always found something wrong with her.

Maybe going through all this would have been easier if Rose had reacted differently about Marisa's kidnapping. Maybe if she'd been able to talk to her mother about everything, she wouldn't be so angry. Not that any of that mattered now. She was never going to have a heart-to-heart with her mother about those awful days and nights.

Sometimes Marisa wondered if her life would have been different if her father hadn't died. She knew he would have loved and supported her throughout the difficult days after the crime. He would have allowed Marisa to talk about what had happened to her. He would have held her if she cried and railed against the injustice.

She shoved these thoughts away and gripped the letter more tightly in her hand. Despite her mother's feelings about it, those sixty days had really happened and it was looking like unless she somehow stopped the perpetrator, it was all going to happen again.

She was just passing a copse of trees when something odd sparked in the sunlight. She frowned and immediately pulled her gun, vaguely surprised that Buddy wasn't reacting to whatever was there.

Slowly she walked closer and tightened her grip on her gun. Her heart thundered as she approached. Whatever it was, it didn't belong.

Then she got close enough to realize it was a truck… Mac's very familiar truck. He wasn't inside, but his guitar case was in the passenger seat.

What was his truck doing parked here? And

where exactly was Mac? She holstered her gun and narrowed her eyes as she continued to walk toward the cabin.

Spirit was out in the corral. "Hey, girl," she said to the horse. "How's my pretty girl today?" As she sweet-talked the horse, she stared at the shed.

Even though Buddy stayed by her side, he was very interested in the shed, as well. He stared at it and his tail thumped with happiness.

How long had Mac been hiding out in the shed? Had he been there for the past five days? Ever since she'd tried to toss him out of her life?

Dammit, Mac was going to screw everything up by trying to play the hero. She didn't need him here. She didn't want him here. If he managed to catch the perpetrator, then she wouldn't have a chance to fulfill her ultimate goal.

A rich anger built up inside her. This was exactly why she had tried to throw him out of her life. She couldn't believe he was here, but he had to go. The last thing she wanted was for Mac to be here when her boogeyman came to call. She drew a deep breath and then stalked into the shed.

Buddy immediately ran to Mac, who was nestled in the hay next to Spirit's stall. He had blankets and a cooler next to him. When he saw her he quickly sat up with a sheepish grin. "Hi, Marisa."

The sight of him and his smile did nothing to abate her anger. It fact, it infuriated her. "Get up,

Mac. Get all your things together and meet me in the cabin." She didn't wait for a reply from him.

She whirled around and headed for the cabin. It was time Mac saw who she really was…it was time she show him the real darkness of her soul.

Mac got up and grabbed the blankets and cooler that had been his constant companions for the past five days and nights. He wasn't sure what had given him away, but he was almost relieved that she'd found him out.

Except for the fact that her nostrils had thinned and her eyes had flashed in a way that let him know she was more than irritated with him. But maybe she would wind up inviting him to stay in the cabin with her instead of him sneaking into her shed.

Surely she couldn't stay angry for too long? He'd shown his utter devotion to keeping her protected and safe. He set his things on the porch stoop and then opened her front door.

She sat in the chair and didn't look any happier to see him now than she had minutes before, when she'd faced him. "How long have you been out in the shed?" she asked without preamble.

He frowned. "For the last five days and nights." He offered her what he hoped was a charming smile. "It would have been much easier and warmer for me if you'd just let me stay in here with you."

"You aren't going to smile your way out of this, Mac. I am so angry with you right now."

His smile fell and he frowned once again. "Why are you so angry with me? All I want to do is keep you safe from harm." She acted like he had committed a cardinal sin against her. "Is there something wrong with that?"

"Yes," she snapped. She got up from the chair. "It's wrong because I didn't ask you for your help. I don't want you staying here with me or camping out in my shed."

"Jeez, Marisa...for God's sake, help me to understand why you don't want me or anyone else to be here to help protect you?"

Her eyes were the color of a turbulent thunderstorm. "I don't want protection from you or anyone else. You know what I want?" She walked over to the sofa and tossed the cushions to the floor, exposing a Taser and a gun. "This is what I want." She walked back to the chair and shoved that cushion off to display a knife and a gun.

She then went to her computer table and pulled a Taser out from beneath it. She did the same at her kitchen table and then whirled back to face him once again.

"Look around, I'm ready for him, Mac. I want him to come and get me and I need to be alone with him." Tears sprung to her eyes. "Please, Mac, you have to leave me be so I can kill him. I want… I need to kill him, Mac."

He stared at all the weapons and then looked at her for a long, stunned moment. Was this the last dark secret she'd hidden from him? He would have never guessed that she had an arsenal of weapons hidden in her furniture and a plan to kill the man she believed had ruined her life.

He took three long strides forward and pulled her into his arms. "Oh, baby," he murmured. She held herself stiffly in his arms and then seemed to sag into his embrace.

He held her as she wept against his chest. He understood her pain. He understood her rage and her feelings of a need for revenge. However, he also believed her high emotions where this horrendous trauma was concerned weren't making her think clearly and rationally.

He ran his hands up and down her back in an effort to soothe her…to calm her. He wished he could magically take her away from all this, to a place of healing and peace where there was no rage or pain.

She finally pushed away from him and angrily swiped at her cheeks. Her gaze when she looked at him was narrow, as if he were her worst enemy.

"Marisa, you don't have to do all this." He gestured to all the weapons she'd revealed. "I understand all the reasons you'd want this man dead, but I can't just stand by and let you face this all alone."

Her brief bout of tears didn't appear to have cooled off her anger. "Why can't you? I don't want Dillon's help and I don't want yours. Why can't you just leave me alone and let me do this my way?"

"I can't," he replied, an irrational anger rising up in him. How could she even ask him to stand down while she met a madman all alone?

"Well, why not?" she half yelled at him, causing Buddy to release a faint growl.

"I can't do that because I'm in love with you." This wasn't exactly the setting he'd had in mind for telling her his innermost feelings, but the words had fallen out of him anyway. "Do you hear me, Marisa? I'm in love with you."

"Well, don't be," she replied frantically as tears once again welled up in her eyes.

"Marisa, the only way I'll stop loving you is if I die. And even then, I will love you through eternity."

Her lower lip trembled. Mac held his breath. Was she going to tell him she was in love with him, too? He believed she was... He believed it with all his heart.

If she would just allow herself to open her heart to him...if she would just allow him to be by her side when the madman came calling, then they could work toward a happy future together.

Her gaze held his for several long moments and then she looked away. "Mac, I want you to go and leave me alone. I don't want you in my house or in my shed." She gazed at him once again and this time her eyes were darkly shuttered and displayed no emotion whatsoever.

"Marisa…"

"Mac, I need you to stay away from me and to respect my choices," she said, cutting him off. "Time is ticking down and this should all be over within the next two weeks. In fact, I got a letter in my mother's mailbox today and I'm sure it's from him."

All of Mac's muscles tightened as a spike of new adrenaline filled him. "What did it say?"

"I don't know. I haven't opened it yet. It's there on the table."

He walked over and picked up the letter, then turned and walked back to her. "Please open it."

She paused a moment and then took the envelope from him. She tore it open and then pulled out the letter inside. *"I'm coming for you, sweet Marisa. I can't wait to get you back in the dark and do horrible things to you. And once I'm done with you, I'll kill you.'"*

She read the words in a monotone and then

placed the letter and the envelope on the love seat's armrest. "That's surprisingly mild for him."

"Mild? He threatened to kill you and you call that mild?" He looked at her incredulously. "We need to call Dillon and give the letter to him. He might be able to pull some fingerprints off it or recognize the handwriting."

"You still don't get it, Mac. I don't want Dillon to arrest him. I don't want you to protect me from him. I want him here, in my cabin, so I can kill him." Her voice shook with emotion.

"Marisa, if you kill him it will change you forever. It will break you," he replied. She had no idea how this kind of action would affect her.

"I'm already broken, Mac. I broke when spending sixty days in hell. Killing him will release me from the control he still has over me, and nobody is going to change my mind."

"So you don't want to call Dillon and give him the letter?" he asked.

"No, I don't."

"Then can I take it to him?"

She picked up the chair cushion and put it back where it belonged. She sat and looked up at him. "Knock yourself out. If that would make you feel better, then feel free to take it with you when you leave. And I want you to leave, Mac. Leave and let me do what I need to do. I also don't want you working with Spirit anymore. But before you go

I need you to promise me you won't hide out in my shed anymore."

God, she was breaking his heart on so many levels right now. He was terrified for her...for not just her physical being, but also for her mental well-being.

She was making a conscious decision to turn her back on him and all the love he had to offer her. She was drowning in the darkness and didn't want anyone to throw her a life jacket. And he so desperately wanted to be her life jacket.

"Promise me, Mac. Promise that you won't be hiding out in my shed anymore."

"I can't change your mind? My love for you isn't enough for you to let me help protect you from harm?" God, his heart was breaking into a million pieces.

"I never wanted you to love me. I was just kicking it with you for a little while, but it was never anything serious. Now please...promise me and then leave," her voice trembled. She stood from the chair and walked over to the door.

Pain squeezed Mac's heart. The way things had been going between the two of them, he'd seen a happy ending for them, but now his hope for that happening hit the floor.

He'd thought she loved him. Even though she hadn't said the actual words, he'd believed that when she was unguarded, he'd seen her love for him shining in her eyes. He'd believed he felt it in her touch, in her kisses whenever they'd made love.

He now realized he'd only been fooling himself. She was just kicking it with him. She didn't really love him; she'd just been passing time with him until the man who haunted her dreams returned for her. He was the man she wanted back in her life.

"I promise I won't hide out in your shed anymore," he finally said.

"Thank you." She opened the door. "If I find you there again, I'll have you charged with trespassing."

Mac swallowed a new gasp at her words. She refused to meet his gaze with hers. "I'll just see you around, Mac," she said.

He couldn't speak. His emotions were far too close to the surface to even try. He grabbed the letter and envelope from the sofa armrest and then left the cabin.

He grabbed the blankets and cooler and headed for his truck parked in the distance. Everything that had happened since she'd found him in the shed seemed surreal…like a bad dream he couldn't awaken from.

He would have never guessed she had an arsenal hidden in her living area. He'd never suspected she intended to meet her monster one-on-one. Finally, he never would have guessed that she didn't love him.

No matter what she believed her wishes were, he was going to take the letter and the envelope to Dillon and hope like hell the lawman would be able to identify the author before he got anywhere close to Marisa.

There was one small ray of hope in his need to protect her. He had promised her that he wouldn't hide out in her shed again, but he'd made no such promise not to hide out behind her cabin.

Chapter 10

For the first time in a week, Marisa left her cabin. With her gun in hand she headed for her car, which she'd parked in her mother's garage. It had been a week since she'd last seen Mac, and the past seven days had been some of the most difficult and emotional days she'd ever had in her entire life.

Sending him away had broken what was left of her heart. She hadn't recognized the absolute depth of her love for Mac until he was gone from her life.

She'd mourned deep and long over the past week. She'd cried for the woman she'd once been, the woman who had a zest for life, and could sleep in the dark without any fears. She'd grieved for the fantasy she'd once envisioned for herself…a future filled with laughter and love and children.

She'd particularly mourned the fact that she would never, could never be the kind of woman that Mac really deserved.

Finally, today, sick of her own company, she'd decided to get out of the cabin and go to the café for lunch. As she passed the copse of trees where she'd discovered Mac's truck a week ago, her heart grew heavy once again.

There was no truck parked there now and in fact she hadn't seen hide nor hair of him in the last week. How was it possible that an empty space beneath some stupid trees could make her feel like crying all over again?

It shouldn't surprise her that he hadn't been around. Not only had she sent him away, but she'd finally shown him who she was when completely unmasked. He'd now seen the ugliness she had inside of her. He'd seen the hatred that burned in her very soul. Once she'd cast him out and he had a little time to think things over, he'd probably breathed a deep sigh of relief that he'd escaped her.

She finally reached her car, tucked her gun into her purse and then headed into town. She was aware of a ticking clock that was heading to a showdown. She'd gotten three more phone calls from *him*. He'd sounded positively gleeful as he'd told her he was coming for her and was going to enjoy his time with her.

Marisa felt him escalating and knew it wouldn't be long now. She was ready for it. She just wanted it to all be over. She'd already destroyed the one wonderful love she would ever find because of her driving need for vengeance.

She hated herself for that. There was a large part of her that wanted to run to Mac's arms. For the first time since those sixty dark days she was starting to doubt herself and her own intentions.

No matter what she chose to do with her kidnapper, she believed she'd done the right thing in pushing Mac away and out of her life. He needed to find a nice woman who was whole, a woman who could sleep with the lights out at night and who had no real baggage. Still, even knowing that was what was best for Mac, imagining him with another woman ripped her up inside.

Her thoughts were so jumbled in her head that she was hoping a little time out of the cabin would help calm them down. As usual the café was busy and she welcomed the noise of silverware clinking and the chatter of people. She needed the chaos to chase away her own thoughts, if only for a little while.

She found an empty two-top table toward the back and claimed it. At least she'd been around town now long enough that nobody stared at her like she had a unicorn horn growing out of the center of her forehead.

She'd just placed her order when Zeke Osmond slid into the chair across from her. "Hey, Marisa."

"Hi, Zeke." Her senses all went on high alert as she gazed at him. "Are you always here at lunchtime?"

He grinned at her. "Most of the time. My boss is a cheapskate who doesn't provide lunch for his ranch hands, although he does provide a decent dinner every night."

"Well, that's good. You work for Raymond Humes, right?"

"That's right," he replied. "I've been working there since I got out of high school. I've been meaning to talk to you but I wasn't sure if it was appropriate." He leaned across the table as if he wanted to tell her a secret.

He smelled rather unpleasant…like sweat and cow dung. "Dillon talked to me about some crazy, anonymous phone calls and notes you've gotten. I just wanted to let you know I had nothing to do with any of them. If I call you or write you something it definitely won't be anonymous."

"Thank you, Zeke," she replied. "I appreciate knowing that."

The conversation paused as the waitress delivered her order of a burger and fries. "Anything else I can get for you?" she asked Marisa with a pleasant smile.

"No, thanks," Marisa replied.

"While I'm here," Zeke continued the minute the waitress had left the table. "I'm on a little vacation from work right now and I was thinking maybe you'd be interested in heading into Oklahoma City with me for a couple of days of fun. Separate hotel rooms, of course," he added hurriedly.

All kinds of alarm bells rang in her head. "Oh, Zeke, thank you for the offer, but I'm really not doing things like that. I have too many things going on to just up and leave town right now."

His beady eyes narrowed slightly but his smile remained on his face. "Oh, well, you can't blame a guy for asking." He stood and glanced over to a nearby table where three men sat. "Looks like my lunch has arrived, too, so I'll just catch up with you later."

"Okay, Zeke. I'll talk to you later." She breathed a sigh of relief as he moved away.

As she ate she thought of the man who had just left her table. He was on vacation… Was he taking those days off because he had a kidnapping in mind?

There was no question in her mind that she found Zeke rather creepy. She knew from Mac that Zeke and a lot of the men from the Humes ranch often caused trouble for the Holiday ranch cowboys. But was Zeke her boogeyman? Was he the man who had taken her and held her for those sixty days of horror?

She'd halfway hoped Mac would be in the café, but he wasn't and that was probably a good thing. She was sure he was back at work on the ranch, where he belonged. She hated that Spirit's training had come to an end, but she couldn't think about that right now. When everything was all over, if she was able, she'd find somebody else to finish up the horse's training.

She'd gone out every afternoon to let Buddy run and so she could talk to her horse. In the past seven days she feared Spirit had regressed a bit, but she hoped Mac would keep his promise that if anything happened to her, he'd take Spirit and Buddy to the Holiday ranch. She knew he would take good care of them.

Her heart broke a little bit at this thought, and again doubts about her plan filled her head. Still, no matter what her future held, she knew Mac wouldn't be a part of it. She loved him too much to bind him to her.

She shoved her plate away, her appetite suddenly gone. She paid her bill and then left the café. She'd hoped this little trip into town would pull her out of her fear…her anxiety…and her utter heartbreak over Mac, but it hadn't worked.

When she got back to her cabin, she curled up on the love seat with Buddy. She turned on her television and stared at the screen. Hot tears burned at her eyes. She'd always prided herself on not being a weepy kind of woman, but in the past seven days she'd cried more tears than she could count.

She wept because her own mother thought she'd done something wrong to warrant the crime against her. She cried because she didn't know why her life had turned out this way. What had she done? Whom had she offended so badly that he wanted her dead?

Finally she cried because she was so damaged, so broken, and she knew in her heart she could never be enough for the man she loved. She would live whatever was left of her life loving Mac to the very depths of her soul, yet knowing she'd done the right thing in breaking things off with him.

"Heading out?" Tucker Caldwell asked Mac as he carried out a couple of blankets and a thermos of coffee from his room. Twilight had just begun to fall and Mac felt the usual urgency he always had at this time of the evening. It was the need to get into place before complete darkness fell.

"Yeah, it's that time of night again," Mac replied.

"And obviously she still hasn't discovered your presence?"

"She doesn't have a clue that I've been camping out behind the cabin each night," Mac replied. He tensed as he thought of what might happen if she did discover him.

"It's such a messed-up situation," Tucker said with a shake of his head.

"All I care about is protecting her from whatever creep is after her." Mac placed the blankets into the back of his pickup, which he'd parked in front of his room in preparation for leaving.

He'd told some of his fellow cowboys about Marisa's desire to just leave things up to Dillon, but he hadn't shared with anyone Marisa's desire to meet the perp alone and try to kill him.

"Dillon doesn't have a clue about who is after her?" Tucker asked.

"No. Whoever this guy is, he was smart enough before not to leave any clues behind, and he's being just as smart this time." Mac sighed in frustration. "And now I'd better get out of here."

"Mac, before you leave…you know any of us would do anything to help out."

Mac smiled. "I know, Tucker, and I appreciate that. But right now there's really nothing you all can do. This is a one-man operation." And if Marisa found out about the one man who was staying on her property, she probably would have him arrested and thrown into jail for trespassing.

It had killed him not to see or talk to her for the past week. The only thing that eased his mind was knowing that he was staying behind her cabin to protect her from evil. Even if she didn't want to ever see him again, he intended to do whatever he could to keep her alive.

He left the ranch and headed toward the Lindale place. As he drove, he thought about the week that had passed. Had she received more phone calls? More threatening notes?

He'd been in touch with Dillon every day and knew she hadn't reported anything new to him. That didn't mean nothing was happening.

For the past week he'd been parking off the beaten path and then hiking into Marisa's cabin from the back of the property. The only people who knew he was doing this were a few of his fellow cowboys and Dillon.

Even though apparently Marisa didn't love him, he still needed to do what his heart told him was right. It wasn't just a want to try to protect her, it was a *need* to try to protect her...as an ex-lover... as a man.

When he reached his hiding place for his truck, he parked and got out. He grabbed everything he'd brought with him and started his hike to the back of the cabin.

From what Marisa had told them about the calls and the notes and the timeline, the perp was coming after her soon. With each step that he took, the urgency to get into place before dark raced through him.

He hadn't cried since his mother had died all those long years ago, but in the last week he'd cried quietly in his room. Marisa's rejection of his love and of his protection had somehow broken a piece of him, and he'd been surprised by the tears of sadness that had found him.

He hadn't picked up his guitar since she'd cast him out of her life. His heart hurt so badly he couldn't hear the music in his own life right now.

Darkness was beginning to fall when he made his little nest of blankets at the back of the cabin. He poured himself a cup of coffee and then stifled a yawn.

Being on guard duty 24/7 was definitely taking a toll on him. His body ached from spending so much time sitting and lying on the hard ground, and tonight his eyes felt gritty from a lack of any real sleep.

He drank a cup of the coffee and then poured himself another one, determined to keep away sleep and spend yet another night on guard duty.

Darkness descended and night insects began to chirp and whirr their night songs. No light came from any of Marisa's windows and it was easy for him to feel like the only person on the face of the earth.

He felt isolated and alone but then he reminded himself of what Marisa must be feeling. She was probably feeling the same way, but with a heavy dose of fear adding to the mix.

As the night deepened, several coyotes howled in the distance. The moon hung low and full with just an occasional cloud to momentarily obscure the silvery illumination.

How many more nights would it take before this all came to a head? Mac would spend a hundred…a thousand more nights hunkered down if it mattered to Marisa's safety.

She had a houseful of weapons, a killer dog and a plan for killing. But the best-laid plans could go awry. There was always the possibility for a mistake to be made, a calculation to be off. And in this case a mistake could mean her disappearance and death. And that thought absolutely terrified him.

She didn't have to love him for him to protect her. She didn't have to want a future with him for him to be on guard for her. It was quite simple. He couldn't just turn off his feelings where she was concerned.

He had no idea what time it was when he suddenly came awake. He must have dozed off. So, what had awakened him? He jerked upright. He saw a shadow in his peripheral vision but before he could react, something hard hit him on the side of his head.

A sharp pain seared through his brain, along with a hundred shooting stars. *Marisa*… Her name was a scream in his head just before everything went black.

His heart beat with utter joy as Mac hit the ground. The cowboy thought he'd been sneaky, hanging out at the back of the cabin, but he'd been on to him.

He'd known Mac needed to be taken out of the mix and he'd done so. Everything was going exactly as planned. Now he had a special dart to neutralize the dog…and then it would be just him and the woman he'd been dreaming about having back in his control.

It was a few minutes after two in the morning. The night was deep and silent. Marisa should be soundly sleeping by now. Maybe she was dreaming of him. He liked that idea. He hoped she was in the midst of a horrendous nightmare where he was her personal demon haunting her nightscape.

He could barely contain his excitement as he left Mac on the ground. Thankfully, with his night vision goggles and the full moon overhead, he didn't need a flashlight to see.

He'd been so safe…so smart so far. He'd worn

gloves each time he'd written and delivered a note to her. Occasionally there had been a police car parked across the street from Rose Lindale's mailbox, but he'd been very careful in making sure he wasn't seen when he put a letter there. He'd also used a different burner phone each time he'd called her.

Almost two years ago he'd fooled the detectives in Oklahoma City and then Dillon Bowie. He'd fooled everyone. He'd walked around among everyone in town. He'd eaten lunch at the café and nobody had known he was the one who had kidnapped Marisa Lindale.

And now it was time to do it all over again. It was finally time to get her back in the dark room in his basement. It was time for her to finally receive the ultimate punishment…humiliation and then death.

Chapter 11

Marisa came awake as Buddy growled. Her heart slammed into her ribs. A glance at her clock on the nightstand let her know it was just after two.

As Buddy jumped off the bed she sat up and reached beneath her pillow and grabbed her gun. She slid from the bed, her heart thundering so loudly she could hear its frantic beat in her head.

Buddy stood at the front door, his hackles raised just as they had been the night the coyotes had come close. A menacing growl issued from the very back of his throat.

Were the coyotes back or was it *him*?

This time was it a two-legged creature causing

Buddy to alert? Was this it…the final confrontation? The timing was right for it to be him. While she didn't know the specifics of how the finale would unfold, she thought she was ready to kill the man who had forever ruined her life.

Her blood chilled her veins with ice as waves of fear rushed through her. She didn't believe it was the coyotes this time. She thought it was a human that had Buddy stirred up. She gripped her gun tightly in her hand as she approached the front door. She drew several deep breaths as she reached for the doorknob.

Buddy would take him down. She wouldn't let Buddy kill the man. She wanted that honor herself. But she hoped Buddy scared the hell out of him. She hoped Buddy bit him hard before she stopped the dog from his attack.

Silently counting to three, she unlocked the door and then threw it open. "Get tough," she said to the dog. Buddy exploded out into the night. Crazy impressions raced through her head in a single second.

The nightscape, with the silvery strands of moonlight dancing down, appeared strange… like the surface of a strange planet she'd never seen before.

Directly ahead, about ten feet away, a sole figure stood. He looked like he belonged in an alien scene. He was clad all in black, the ski mask and night goggles making him appear as if he was from another galaxy.

Buddy flew toward him, snarling and gnashing his teeth. She froze as the man raised a weapon. *Pssst.* The strange sound was followed by Buddy's yip. Buddy immediately fell to the ground. He yipped a few more times and then fell silent.

"No!" she screamed. Oh God…a knife sliced painfully through her heart. She'd made up several scenarios in her head, but in none of them was Buddy hurt or killed. She'd always assumed Buddy would surprise the man and take him down before the man could react.

Before she could compose herself, the man rushed her and hit her with enough force to knock her backward to the floor. Her head took a hard blow and her gun skittered away from her hand.

Then he turned off the light.

The room was plunged into darkness and his sick, familiar laughter filled the air. For a moment the darkness completely disoriented her. The back of her throat closed up and she gasped for breath.

The dark…oh God, it surrounded her, it invaded her very soul. She couldn't think. She couldn't move. She was frozen in place, her frantic heartbeat the only sound she could hear.

And then he touched her.

She jumped and screamed at the feel of the hand stroking her hair. His laughter filled the cabin once again, the maniacal sound of the devil's mirth.

The sound broke her inertia. She had to get to her room. There was a light in there and she needed her night vision goggles and another weapon. He laughed again and a new terror shot through her.

This wasn't the way it was supposed to happen. Once again she was scrabbling along the floor in the dark to find some semblance of safety.

She knew he could see her, but she couldn't see him. Flashbacks of her time in captivity seared through her mind. He could grab her…hit her or shoot her at any moment. And she couldn't even think of Buddy right now or she'd just curl up in a fetal ball and give up.

She wished Mac was here. She was sorry now that she'd sent him away. She'd thought she could face all this alone, but she couldn't. She was scared and she just wanted all this to end.

"Where are you going, Marisa?" His voice was familiar, but she couldn't quite place it. He laughed again. "There's no place to run, no place to hide from me."

He was toying with her. She needed to get to her room and grab the night goggles. Then if he managed to douse the bedside lamp in the bedroom, the fight would be more fair.

She didn't have another gun in her bedroom,

but she did have a Taser. All she needed was a chance to use it. If she could, then hopefully he would be incapacitated long enough for her to grab a gun from the living room.

She finally made it to her bedroom door. She rose to her feet and threw it open. The light from her nightstand lamp breathed new life into her.

She raced to the nightstand and grabbed the goggles. She threw a glance over her shoulder, grateful that he wasn't anywhere in sight. He was someplace in the dark, waiting for her.

Pulling on her goggles, she tried to calm some of the fear that torched through her. She needed to be cool and composed to complete this mission. She grabbed the Taser and gripped it tightly.

There was no room for failure. This was why she'd turned her back on Mac. This was what she'd prepared herself for, and the time was now.

Suddenly he was in the doorway with his gun pointing directly at her. Her heart banged hard. This had been a deadly miscalculation. She hadn't anticipated him killing Buddy or rushing her so quickly that she'd lose her gun. She hadn't expected the darkness and now he was going to kill her.

He suddenly whirled to the right and shot out the lamp on her nightstand, plunging the room into darkness. Through her night goggles she saw him step back out of the room.

"Let's play, Marisa," he called out. "Let's play a little game of hide-and-seek."

Tears burned at her eyes. She didn't want to play a game. She just wanted this over and done. She never wanted to think about this man again. She desperately wanted this poison out of her life forever.

She drew a deep breath and whirled out of the bedroom door, the Taser leading the way. Before she could find him, he slammed into her back. She fell to her knees and crawled away as quickly as she could.

"Now, that's what I like to see," he said gleefully. "Crawl on the floor and grovel at my feet."

Her knees hurt and her head still ached from coming into hard contact with the floor moments before. Still she rose to her feet. The goggles only helped a little bit in the dark. Initially she didn't see him.

A bullet flew to the left of her, the sound exploding so loudly it hurt her ears. She hit the floor and rolled to her side. Then she saw him just behind the love seat.

Again she realized he was toying with her. He'd had a perfect shot at her and hadn't taken it. He didn't want her dead. He wanted to take her back to where she'd been before…in his dark lair. She would rather die than live in the dark with him again.

He moved along the floor, his laughter once again ringing out. As long as he was there she couldn't get to the weapons the love seat hid and she couldn't shoot him with the Taser.

"Marisa…sweet Marisa." Once again his voice sounded familiar.

Who was he? She wanted to rip his ski mask off and see his face. She needed to know who this man was that had destroyed her and still filled her with such fear.

"What are you waiting for, you bastard?" she screamed. "Come after me, you crazy jerk. If you want me so badly, then quit hiding and come for me."

"With pleasure." He rose and for the first time she saw he also had a Taser in his hand. He shot at her and she dove to the right, at the same time firing off hers.

Direct hit. With a scream he hit the floor. The Taser discharge lasted about five seconds, and in those seconds his muscles jumped and spasmed. She approached where he had fallen and kicked both his gun and the Taser away from him.

She shot him again with the Taser and then grabbed the chair cushion, threw it on the floor and picked up the gun that had been hidden there. She pointed it at the man sprawled on the floor and reached behind her with the other hand to flip on the light switch.

The overhead ceiling light filled the room with bright illumination. She yanked her goggles off and threw them on the love seat.

He finally managed to sit up. "Well played, Marisa."

She stared at him. "Take off your goggles and mask," she said, surprised by the tremble in her voice…the tremble in her gun hand. This was what she'd waited for…what she'd worked for, wasn't it?

At that moment the front door exploded inward and Mac flew inside, a gun in his hand. In one quick minute he took in the scene before him.

"Take off your goggles and mask," she repeated. She didn't know how Mac had managed to be here at this exact moment in time, but right now it didn't matter. Nothing else mattered except the creep on the floor.

She didn't look at Mac. Instead she looked at the man who had haunted her dreams. "Take them off because I need to see who, exactly, I'm going to kill."

"Do as she says," Mac said from just behind her.

Wasn't he going to stop her? Try to talk her out of what she intended to do now? Mac knew she intended to kill the man. The perp slowly took off his goggles. "Now, the ski mask," she said.

She held her breath. Finally she was going to

see her monster. She would be face-to-face with the man who had destroyed her, a man who had made her afraid of the dark and had broken her.

He paused with one hand holding the bottom of the mask. Her heart beat a frantic rhythm. Was it Zeke Osmond behind the mask? Brendon? They all had a similar body type.

As he began to pull off the mask, she held her breath. With one big yank, he was revealed. She gasped in surprise and heard Mac's gasp from behind her.

"Joe," she said in stunned surprise. Joe Mills... the boy who had dropped out of high school, the man who had changed out her battery. He was the one who had kidnapped her? Held her and tormented her in the dark for sixty long days?

"Joe...why?" The single question fell from her lips as she continued to stare at him in disbelief. He hadn't even been on her radar.

"Why?" He laughed, that wicked sound that shot shivers through her. His laughter stopped and his eyes burned with hatred. "I'll tell you why... because you had your nose so far up in the air you didn't even notice me. You didn't notice how much I loved you in high school."

"Loved me? You dropped out of high school," she replied, her head still reeling.

"I dropped out because of you," he screamed. "I couldn't stand to see you every minute of the day and not have you, but dropping out only made it worse." He started to rise but she took a step closer to him and cocked the gun pointed at his chest.

"When you left for Oklahoma City my love for you turned to hate. I hate you, Marisa. I hate you so much. The best days of my life were when I had you in my control so I could humiliate you. You left me when I needed you most, when I was little and scared."

What? What was he talking about? When he was little? He shook his head and narrowed his eyes. "If I had the chance I'd do it all over again. I would lock you up in the dark and poke you and watch you scrabble naked across the bare floor."

"Shut up," she said. Her anger rose up as she remembered what she'd endured as a captive.

"Shoot me," Joe said. "You want to kill me? You hate me like I hate you. We're the same, Marisa. I would have killed you if I got the chance to have you again, so shoot me."

This was what she'd planned for...what she had dreamed would happen. The man who had tortured her, who had ruined her was now here before her, helpless and at her mercy.

"Dillon is on his way," Mac said.

She started at the sound of his deep voice. She'd forgotten he was just behind her.

She stared at Joe. She'd dreamed of killing the man who had ruined her life. Now was her chance.

Her hand was sweaty around the gun. *Just shoot him*, a loud voice in her head demanded. *This is exactly what you wanted, the moment you've waited for.*

Yet a little voice whispered that killing him would never give her back those sixty days. Killing him wouldn't allow her to sleep with the lights off.

A siren sounded in the distance. Dillon would be here within minutes. *Kill him*, the loud voice in her head screamed. Sweat broke out and her breathing became shallow, making her feel half-nauseous.

Just pull the trigger. Kill him like he killed you. And another voice said, *Don't be like him. You don't have to kill him to get justice.* The two voices in her head warred with each other.

Tears fell from her eyes, half blinding her. For the first time since her ordeal had begun she realized she didn't really want to kill him. She didn't want that additional stain on her soul. She just wanted him gone from her life forever.

She dropped her arm and turned to Mac. "Watch him until Dillon gets here."

She stepped around Mac and strode outside. The night was cold, but she didn't care. She needed to get to Buddy and tell her faithful companion goodbye.

As she approached where he had fallen, sobs

began to choke her. She'd gotten her bad guy, but at what cost? Her whole idea had been stupid and her stupidity had gotten Buddy killed. He'd given his life for her, but she wanted him back. She should have never put somebody she loved in this kind of danger.

Dillon and a deputy she didn't recognize pulled in at the same time she collapsed on the ground next to Buddy. "Where is he?" Dillon yelled. She pointed to the cabin and then wrapped her arms around her sweet, furry and faithful dog.

Despite the cold of the night, his body was still warm. She buried her face in his fur and cried. What had she done? In the blindness of her hatred she'd destroyed everything and caused Buddy to die. "I'm sorry, Buddy. I'm so sorry," she sobbed.

She was vaguely aware of Dillon escorting a handcuffed Joe out of the cabin and to his car. Following right behind was Mac, who immediately hurried toward her.

At that moment, she thought she felt Buddy take a breath. Was it just wishful thinking? She leaned her face down by his nose and felt his faint breathing.

"Mac! Mac, he's still alive. We need to get him to the vet right away." Tears chased down her cheeks. Was there hope, or was it already too late?

"Marisa, your car is closer than my truck." He

leaned down and gently picked Buddy up in his arms. "Dillon can take us up to the house."

Dillon got out of his car and told Marisa to get behind the wheel of his running vehicle. "This perp and I can walk up to the house. Go."

Within seconds Marisa was roaring up the lane toward her mother's house as she continued to cry. It took them only minutes to change into Marisa's car and then she headed to Dr. Dan Richards's house, where he had his veterinary office in the back.

Mac continued to hold Buddy in his arms and she could hear him talking softly to the dog. "Come on, Buddy. You hang on. We're going to get you help."

When they arrived at the vet's house, she jumped out of the car and banged on the office door. Mac joined her at the door with Buddy in his arms.

Dr. Richards came to the door and gestured them inside. He had Mac carry the dog into an examining room where Mac placed him on a table.

In between sobs, Marisa explained what had happened to Buddy, that she didn't know what Joe had shot him with. "Let me run some blood work and other tests. You two go back out to the waiting room. This will take a little while."

Marisa collapsed into one of the plastic chairs in the waiting room and was acutely aware of Mac sitting next to her. "He's got to be okay...he just has to be," she exclaimed as she swiped at her tear-stained cheeks.

"He's a strong boy and I'm sure he's fighting to stay with you." Mac wrapped an arm around her, but she remained stiff and not yielding to the desire to melt into him.

"If Joe poisoned him, then he might not pull through," she replied and a new wave of tears fell from her eyes. "It's all my fault. I've been so stupid."

"Don't beat yourself up. Dr. Dan is good at what he does. If anyone can pull Buddy through, he can." Mac pulled her closer and she finally succumbed to the need to lean into him and feel his warmth battle with the iciness that still encased her heart.

It felt like an eternity before the vet finally stepped back into the waiting room. Both Marisa and Mac bolted out of their chairs.

"Is he going to be all right?" Marisa asked desperately.

Dan smiled. "He's going to be just fine. As far as I can tell he was tranquilized and not poisoned."

Marisa nearly fell to her knees in relief. "Oh, thank God. So, what happens next?"

"I'd like to keep him here at least for the rest of the night and tomorrow. I'm giving him intravenous fluids and I'll continue to monitor his vital signs. You can call me tomorrow afternoon and we'll see where we are."

"Thank you," Marisa said, her eyes filling with tears of relief this time.

Minutes later they were again in Marisa's car and headed back to her mother's place. As the adrenaline left her, she just felt numb, but she still had some questions for Mac.

"How did you know?" she asked after several moments of silence. "How were you there at the same time Joe was there?"

"I've been camping out behind your cabin. Unfortunately, he must have known I was there. He hit me over the head and knocked me unconscious. I'm not sure how long I was out before I came to and ran into the cabin," he explained.

"So you've been there all along."

"Marisa, I couldn't leave you alone," he replied softly. "I wanted to be there when he came for you."

"Why didn't you try to stop me from killing Joe?"

"I knew when it came right down to it, you wouldn't."

She glanced over to him. "How did you know that?"

His smile was visible in the light from the dashboard. "Because I know who you are in your heart and soul."

She looked back out at the road, feeling like she wanted to cry all over again.

"How are you feeling now that it's all over?"

She drew in a deep breath and released it on a sigh. "I am physically and emotionally completely exhausted." It was the truth. Now that she knew Buddy was taken care of and her monster was in jail, all she wanted to do was go to sleep.

She pulled into her mother's garage and reached beneath her car seat for a flashlight she kept there. She had to walk to her cabin from here and it was still dark outside.

"Where is your truck?" she asked when they exited the garage.

"I'm parked off the main road behind your cabin. I'll walk you to your door."

They fell into step side by side, the full moon casting down more light to add to the beam of her flashlight. At least she didn't have to worry anymore about her boogeyman jumping out to carry her away.

She still couldn't believe it had been Joe Mills. She had a feeling she'd hear more about him and the original crime perpetrated against her once Dillon finished his investigation.

She was grateful that Mac remained quiet. She didn't want to talk. She didn't even want to think. Nothing had really changed in her mind where the two of them were concerned.

They finally reached her front door and she turned to look at him. "Thank you, Mac. I appreciate everything you did to try to keep me safe."

"And you didn't even need me. You handled it all by yourself. It's over now and you can finally really move forward with your life." He stuck his hands in his pockets. "Marisa... I..."

"Mac, I'm really exhausted," she said, interrupting whatever he was about to say. "Thank you again and I'll touch base with you later."

She didn't wait for a response and instead quickly stepped inside and closed and locked the door. A rush of emotions crashed in on her and she went directly into her bedroom and collapsed on the bed.

All her emotions rose up inside her, a tangled mix of residual fear, of grief over Buddy and finally heartbreak about Mac. Yes, her ordeal was finally over. Joe would be facing a number of charges and probably go away to prison for a very long time. According to Dr. Dan, Buddy was going to be okay and her mission for justice was over.

And then there was Mac. Her heart constricted with thoughts of him. He'd won her heart in so many ways...from the warmth of his eyes when he gazed at her to his gentle touch and sweet music.

But he would not be part of her future going forward. She had to release him so he could find the kind of woman he really deserved. Even though her ordeal was over she was still damaged goods.

Mac deserved a woman who could sleep with the lights out and she didn't know if she would, if she ever could, be that woman. She had to let him go.

Chapter 12

It was not only Thanksgiving Day, but also a reunion day. Cassie, along with Dusty's help, had
arranged for all the lost boys to come together
to the enormous feast that Cookie had prepared.

The barn was filled with all the cowboys and
their wives, and toddlers and babies were every-
where. Laughter rang out in the room, which was
redolent with the scents of turkey and ham, stuffing and candied sweet potatoes, just to name a few
of the dishes on the buffet table.

Mac was happy to see the men he'd grown up
with, men he considered his brothers, but there
was a core of grief in his heart that took away
some of the pleasure of the late-afternoon meal.

It had been five days since Joe Mills was arrested, five long days since he'd seen Marisa. He'd called her the day after the arrest and she'd been brisk and stiffly polite to him. He'd called her the next day and invited her to the Thanksgiving meal. She'd declined and told him it was time he stopped calling her, that she was moving on with her life.

He'd ended the call by telling her that if she changed her mind, dinner was at five. As the time to eat grew closer, he'd hoped to see her walk through the door.

When they were all finally filling plates from the buffet Cookie had set up, he had to admit defeat. She was not coming and apparently any relationship he'd thought they shared had only been a dream.

It had been a wonderful dream...his very best dream. She was the woman he wanted in his life forever, but if he wasn't her forever man then there was no hope for a future between them.

He was surrounded by loving couples and laughing children, which only made the absence of Marisa more painful. "Hey, Lucas, how's that ranch of yours getting along?" Flint asked. Lucas Taylor had been the first of them to find love with Nicolette, Cassie's best friend who had come with her when Cassie took over the ranch.

"Things are going great," Lucas replied. "In

fact, I'm making so much money I could probably hire Forest to come work for me. Unfortunately I wouldn't be able to afford to feed him."

Forest looked up from the heaped plate he had just filled. "Ha ha, like I haven't heard those jokes before from you clowns."

That set the mood through the meal. The boys who had grown up to be men together teased each other unmercifully. They talked about good memories and commiserated over bad.

They all teased Mac about being the last single cowboy, their good-natured jabs piercing straight through his broken heart.

The evening wound down and somebody yelled for Mac to play his guitar. He grabbed it from where he had leaned it against a wall earlier.

He sat and began to strum and everyone fell silent. He played a couple of tunes and then began to play the old songs that they all used to sing together.

As the men began to sing, a real sense of community filled the barn. No matter where they all lived, no matter where their futures took them, Mac would never forget the eleven men he'd grown up with.

He even found himself thinking about Adam. He'd been one of the boys, but none of them had known about the darkness inside him. And that darkness had resulted in him committing murder and then being killed.

However, no matter how warm he felt in the company of his "brothers," there was still a core of icy loneliness in his soul.

He'd really hoped that with Joe Mills behind bars, Marisa would be able to accept all the love he had for her…and recognize that she loved him, too. He'd imagined that once her ordeal was finally over they would be talking about marriage and children, but instead she wasn't talking to him at all.

He felt like his music would never be as good as it had been when it was just the two of them sitting in front of Spirit's corral. His life would never be as good as on those nights he'd fallen asleep with her in his arms.

Still, it had been a heartwarming day with all of them together once again. Darkness had fallen by the time Mac quit playing.

Cassie stood and everyone fell silent. "I just want to say that there's a lot of love in this barn and I'm so glad that we could all spend this holiday together as Big Cass's family. She would have loved having her boys all here back together again."

She cleared her throat, obviously overcome with emotion, and then began again. "You all know how much you meant to her and to me. And

I've loved having us all together again today. As you all go back to your lives, I wish you safe travel and know that you'll always have a place here on the Holiday ranch."

A side barn door flew open with enough force to shake the building. Tucker stepped in, a frantic look on his face. "Fire," he yelled. "The stable is on fire."

All the men jumped up and headed for the doors. Fire? In the stable? All Mac could think about was the horses. He had to get them all out. He had to save the horses.

As he ran out of the barn and into the darkness he looked at the stable and his heart thundered frantically. It wasn't just a small fire like they'd had in the past. Bright flames shot up toward the sky.

Forest raced alongside Mac while the other men ran to the stations they'd been assigned as young boys in case something like this happened.

Big Cass had made sure there were water sources all over the property. She'd known that being so far away from town she wouldn't be able to depend on the volunteer fire department and that a fire could quickly destroy a ranch.

By the time Mac and Forest entered the stable the entire structure was filled with black, noxious smoke. "I'll let them out of the stalls and you guide them into the pasture," Mac yelled.

"Got it," Forest replied.

As Mac ran to the stalls that were closest to the fire, he could feel the scorching heat on his face. His eyes began to burn and water uncontrollably. His lungs burned and he began to cough.

Despite his intense physical discomfort, his desire to get to the horses was a desperate need. The animals were whinnying with fear. Their eyes rolled wildly as they kicked and reared up in their stalls.

He raced to the first stall and threw it open, but the horse…Dusty's horse…refused to come out. He stepped around to the back of the horse and shoved the big animal, yelling loudly. Finally the horse bolted out and Mac moved to the next stall.

His head began to pound as the soot-filled air grew more and more difficult to breathe. As each horse ran outside, Forest guided them through the gate and into the open pasture.

The fire was growing bigger and the heat more intense, but Mac didn't stop until every single horse was out safely.

He finally stumbled out of the burning building and bent over as a series of harsh coughs racked his body. He straightened and stared around him. The other men, who were silhouetted by the fire in the otherwise dark night, shouted to each other as some of them directed streams of water from hoses and others wielded fire extinguishers.

Behind the stable was a wooded area. Still coughing and feeling light-headed, Mac walked over toward the woods. He just needed to sit for a moment and try to catch his breath. He was about to sink down in the grass when something caught his eye.

It was a figure moving away from the stables with a flashlight and what appeared to be a gas can in his hand. A new burst of adrenaline shot through Mac. "Hey," Mac yelled. The man shot a glance backward and Mac recognized him.

Zeke Osmond. Mac wondered how many other men from the Humes ranch were running around in the woods and away from the Holiday ranch like rats abandoning a burning ship.

"Stop," Mac yelled as he raced after Zeke. He needed to stop him from getting away. If he could catch Zeke and hold him for arrest, then finally at least one of the guilty would get a taste of justice.

Mac pushed himself faster, his lungs burning with his efforts. He coughed and coughed from the smoke he had inhaled in the stable. His head pounded with a nauseating intensity.

He finally got close enough to leap and tackle Zeke from behind. As the two hit the ground, Mac was vaguely aware of two things… Forest was there with him and Zeke, and Mac was going to pass out.

As Forest took control of Zeke, Mac rolled over

on his back, and even though someplace in the back of his mind he knew it was impossible to see the stars through the smoke, he saw them. They all swirled around and suddenly a vision of Marisa filled his head and then he knew no more.

Mac awakened to find himself in a hospital bed. Early-morning light filtered through the window blinds and he was surprised to find himself hooked up to an oxygen tank.

That was when he remembered...the stable fire, a painful burning in his lungs and chasing after Zeke. What had happened after that? Apparently he'd collapsed, but had the stables burned down? Had Zeke been arrested?

Or had he been shot? Had Zeke managed to put a bullet in him before he got away? Mac mentally checked for any pain in his body. There was none. Surely if he'd been shot he would feel some kind of pain. And he didn't hurt except for a slight sore throat.

He didn't know how long he was in the room alone when Megan Pierson walked in. Megan was in her thirties, a nice-looking woman Mac had dated a couple of times. Thankfully, they had both agreed they didn't belong together and had parted ways quite amicably.

"Mac McBride...what have you done to yourself now?" she said in greeting.

"I'm not sure. You're going to have to tell me," he replied. "Last I remember I was chasing Zeke Osmond through the woods, and then I woke up here."

"I heard there was also a fire out at Cassie's place."

Mac frowned. "Have you heard how bad the fire was?"

"No, I'm sorry, I haven't. What I'm going to do now is chart your vitals and then I'll see what I can tell you."

She took his temperature and blood pressure, and checked his oxygen level. She charted them into a little computer on wheels and then smiled at him. "Okay, so how are you feeling this morning?" she asked.

"I'm feeling just fine," Mac replied.

"I can tell by the hoarseness in your voice that you can't be feeling just fine," Megan chided him.

"Okay, I'll admit I have a bit of a sore throat."

Megan nodded. "You were brought in last night for smoke inhalation, which is why you are under oxygen right now," she explained.

"So, when can I get out of here?" he asked, eager to get back home and find out how bad the damage had been to the stable and if anyone had been arrested.

"I can't tell you that, but the doctor should be in soon. Until then I'll let the kitchen staff know you're awake and they'll rustle you up some breakfast."

"Sounds good," he replied.

He was definitely hungry. It seemed like it had been a long time ago that he had enjoyed the Thanksgiving feast with all his "brothers."

Thank goodness those men had all been there to help with the fire. They had worked together like they had when they'd been Big Cass's boys.

He wondered if Marisa had heard about the fire. If so, had she worried about him? Had she wondered about his safety? He shoved these thoughts aside as his breakfast tray arrived. The painful truth was she wasn't his to think about anymore.

He had just finished his meal of scrambled eggs, toast and bacon when Dillon walked in. "Hey, Mac...how are you doing?"

"Physically I think I'm fine, but I have a lot of questions for you. How bad was the fire?"

Dillon frowned. "About a fourth of the building is either ashes or badly smoke-damaged, but the good news is, thanks to you I not only arrested Zeke, but Sawyer caught Lloyd Green and we got two others from the Humes ranch for arson."

"And you have the evidence to put them away?" Mac asked.

Dillon smiled. "I do. They were all stupid enough to either be caught with a gas can in their hands, or drop the cans with their fingerprints all over them. Finally I'll get a little justice for at least part of the criminal activity they've done to us over the years."

"That's great news. So, was anyone from the ranch hurt?" Mac asked.

"Only one knucklehead who decided to run into a burning building filled with smoke," Dillon replied with another grin. "But thanks to your efforts, we didn't lose a single horse. You got them all out safe and sound."

"Now, that's real music to my ears."

"And you're off duty for the rest of the week. I don't want to see you doing any kind of work at the ranch for the next seven days. And that stands even if the doctor releases you with a clean bill of health."

"Okay, but you know that's probably not necessary," Mac replied. "I'm feeling just fine."

"According to Cassie and me, it's necessary. Well, I just wanted to stop by and see how you are doing," Dillon said.

"I'm hoping once the doctor gets in here I'll be on my way home."

"That's good. I'll see you later, Mac."

Once Dillon left, the visitors began to stream in. Lucas Taylor and his wife, Nicolette, started the parade. Next was Nick Coleman and Adrienne, and then Forest and Patience.

These were all men who didn't work on the Holiday ranch anymore. Mac knew the men who worked on the ranch would all be busy, after the fire the night before. They would need to get a new stable up before winter really hit.

Finally Dr. Clayton Rivers came into the room. "Hi, Mac. I suppose you're chomping at the bit to get out of here."

"You've got that right," Mac replied.

"First of all, let's get that oxygen off you." Dr. Clayton removed the tubing from Mac's nostrils. He then listened to Mac's lungs. "Sounds good," he proclaimed. "So, how are you feeling? Any issues? I can tell you're a little hoarse. Does your throat hurt?"

"Just a little bit."

"That's because of all the smoke you inhaled last night. It should be fine in the next day or two. And you need to rest not only your throat, but also yourself."

"I can do that," Mac readily replied.

"You sit tight for now and I'll start working on your discharge paperwork. Once it's finished I'll send Megan in." He turned to leave the room and practically bumped into Marisa coming in.

Mac's heart jumped with wild joy at the sight of her. She looked positively beautiful in a pair of jeans and a royal blue sweater that enhanced her dark hair and blue-gray eyes. "Marisa." Her name fell softly from his lips.

She took two steps into the room, looking awkward and ill at ease. "Hi, Mac, I heard about the fire last night and I…uh…just wanted to come by and make sure you were okay."

For a brief moment he merely drank in the sight of her. It felt as if it had been months and months since he'd seen her, since they had been in each other's presence.

"I'm fine," he finally said. "In fact I'm going to be released here in just a few minutes."

"You don't sound fine," she replied as a frown flitted across her forehead.

"I'm just a bit hoarse from the smoke I inhaled, but it should be gone in the next day or two. How have you been?" He searched her features as if he needed to memorize them for a lifetime. Who knew when he might be in a room alone with her again?

"I've been okay."

An awkward silence fell between them. He continued to look at her and she looked everyplace in the room but at him. Finally she looked at him again. "Uh… I was actually wondering if you could maybe start working with Spirit again. She's regressed a bit and I'm worried about her."

She held his gaze for a moment and then glanced away once again.

His heart leaped at this new opportunity to spend time with Spirit and her owner. "Marisa, you know I'll work with her again. How about later today…maybe around five?"

"Are you sure you feel up to it?" She gazed at him once again.

"Trust me, I feel just fine. I apparently just had a little smoke inhalation issue going on last night." She obviously had no idea that if he had a broken leg and was half-blind he'd still show up for an opportunity to be around her.

"You could have been killed." Her eyes flashed with an emotion he couldn't quite identify.

"But I wasn't and I'm fine and I'll look forward to seeing you and Spirit later today."

"Thanks, Mac, and I'm glad you're okay." She quickly turned and left his room.

Mac stared after her. There was no question it had been an odd encounter. For most of the time she'd given off the energy of a reluctant visitor. He was surprised she was inviting him back to work with Spirit.

Was her invitation a beginning to a new and better relationship with him? He hoped so. He wanted that so badly. However, he knew he had to somehow hang on to his heart. This might only be an invitation to heartbreak once again.

* * *

Marisa stood by the corral, her heart beating a crazy rhythm of anticipation. She'd already pulled out the two chairs, and Buddy stood by her side. Thankfully, there were no long-term effects from the tranquilizer Joe Mills had used, and Buddy was back to his normal, wonderful self.

She'd been terrified when her mother had called her early that morning to tell her there had been a fire at the Holiday ranch and that Mac had been taken to the hospital.

She felt as if she'd stopped breathing as she thought of a world without Mac McBride in it. She'd needed to see for herself how he was doing. She'd been relieved to make the quick hospital visit that had assured her he was okay.

Over the past week she'd tried to not think about Mac. She'd come out every day and talked to Spirit, but realized she still needed help with the horse.

One minute she'd thought about calling Mac and the next moment she'd decided to call somebody else to finish the work with the horse. She'd even looked online to see who else lived in the area and trained horses. She found fault with each and every one of them.

Ultimately she'd decided that Mac was the only person she really trusted. She wanted him to work with Spirit until a trainer was no longer needed.

She was hoping to go back to her original plan… to have Mac just be a man who trained her horse and nothing more. She couldn't let it be more. She would never be the kind of woman he deserved and that was the end of it.

Still, she couldn't help the way her heart jumped as she saw his truck approaching down the lane toward her cabin. He would only have a couple of hours to work as the sun set early in the evenings.

Despite the fact that Joe was in jail, her fear of the dark hadn't magically disappeared. She had no idea if or when she'd ever feel comfortable to be outside in the darkness of the night.

Mac pulled up and parked, then got out of the truck with his guitar case in his hand and that warm smile curving his lips. Her heart squeezed so tight at the sight of him she could scarcely breathe.

"Hey, Marisa," he said. "I see you have the chairs all ready for us."

"Yes, I figured I could do at least that much." She watched as he leaned the guitar case against the corral railing. Buddy ran to him, obviously looking for some extra love from him.

Mac laughed and leaned down on one knee to greet Buddy and scratch him behind the ears. "It's so good to see you, Buddy," he said and then stood. "I'm glad to see him back to his normal self."

She smiled. "It took two days for him to really bounce back, but thankfully he has a clean bill of health and is back where he belongs." She sobered. "How are you feeling?"

"I'm feeling just fine. I finally got back to the ranch about two hours ago. Of course, seeing the burned stable there made me absolutely sick."

"I heard Zeke was one of the men arrested," she replied. The conversation felt slightly stilted. There were so many other things she wished she could say to him, so many things that were locked away in her heart because they had to be.

"We've always known Zeke and a few of his pals were troublemakers. I'm just happy that last night they finally got caught. Maybe a little time in jail will make them all finally leave us alone."

"That would be nice," she replied.

She watched as he leaned against the corral railings and called to Spirit. He was such a handsome man, and as he sweet-talked the horse she found herself swallowing the emotions that threatened to rise to the surface.

Mac turned and gazed at her. "How about a few tunes before we head into the corral?"

"Sounds good," she agreed. He grabbed his guitar and they sat side by side in the chairs. As he began to play a slow country-Western song, the sweet notes rode the air and Spirit walked to the railing to gaze at them with her soft brown eyes.

Marisa closed her eyes. This was what she would remember for the rest of her life…this time with Buddy lazing in the grass and Spirit looking relaxed and at peace as a man she loved played his guitar.

She would always hold in her heart these moments when a handsome cowboy sat next to her, his scent and his warmth giving her a sense of peace and security she would probably never find again. She felt safe here with him. She'd always felt secure and happy with him. She'd always felt as if she belonged with him.

When he began to play his second song and added his voice, the emotions she'd tamped down bubbled to the surface. Tears began to seep from her eyes. She wanted this so badly…she wanted him so badly.

She tried desperately to gain some control, but her tears kept coming. Suddenly the music stopped and in the resulting silence, a small sob escaped her.

"Marisa? Are you crying?" Mac's slightly hoarse, soft voice, so filled with obvious concern, pierced through to her very soul.

"Of course not." She tried to play it off, but another sob hiccuped out of her.

"But you are," Mac replied. He set the guitar

aside and moved his chair closer to hers. "You want to talk about it?"

"No," she replied. She squeezed her eyes tightly closed.

"Marisa, it's obvious something is wrong. You know you can talk to me about anything."

"I...I can't tell you what I really want to tell you," she managed to gasp out.

"Have I done something wrong? Marisa, you know I would never intentionally do anything to upset you."

"I know," she replied and cried even harder. She was so embarrassed and shocked by her utter lack of control.

"Well, obviously something is wrong." He got up from his chair and reached for her hand. Weak with her emotions, she allowed him to pull her up and out of her chair.

"Talk to me, Marisa." His gentle brown eyes searched her features, obviously seeking answers for her tears. "Talk to me and let me help fix whatever is making you cry."

"You can't fix it for me," she replied.

"So tell me what's really going on, Marisa. Buddy is good and healthy and Spirit is going to be a great horse, and Joe Mills is probably going to spend the rest of his life in prison."

"I know...everything should be wonderful, but it's not...because I'm in love with you." She slapped a hand over her traitorous mouth and stepped back from him.

His eyes widened and then his beautiful smile curved his lips. "Why doesn't that make everything wonderful? You know how much I love you, Marisa. I want to lay my head down beside yours every night and wake up with you in my arms every morning…every day for the rest of my life. I want to marry you and call you my wife. I want you to hold our babies in your arms while I sing them lullabies."

He reached toward her but she took another step backward, each one of his words only breaking her heart more. "Don't you get it, Mac? I want all that with you, too, but I'm too broken. It's possible I'll have to sleep with the lights on for the rest of my life. My own mother doesn't even find me worthy of her love and attention. It's probably always going to be hard for me to trust people."

"First of all, that's your mother's issue and not yours, Marisa," he replied. "From what you've told me about her and from what I know about her, she's definitely the one who is broken."

He took another step toward her, but still she retreated from him, stumbling back a step. "Marisa, I'll sleep in the light with you anytime. It's nice to know that if I were to wake up I'd be able to see your beautiful face. As far as trusting anyone, as long as you trust me, that's all that's really important."

Once again he reached out and this time she didn't step back from him. He placed his hands on her shoulders and gazed at her with an intensity that half stole her breath away.

"Marisa, this past week of not seeing you has been the longest week in my entire life. You're the first thing I think about in the mornings and the last thing I think about before I go to sleep. Give me a chance, Marisa. Give us a chance."

"You deserve better, Mac. I'm just so…so broken."

He placed his fingers under her chin and raised her face. "You're only as broken as you tell yourself you are. You may feel broken, but you're absolutely perfect for me. You've had enough sadness in your life, Marisa. Let me make you happy."

"You already do make me happy." She stared into the very depths of his eyes.

"Marry me, Marisa. Marry me and make me the happiest man on the face of the earth."

Was it possible? When she gazed into his loving eyes, all things seemed possible. Was it really possible she wasn't as broken as she thought herself to be? Joe Mills had already taken away so much of her life. Was she going to allow him to take away more?

"Are you really sure you want me, Mac?"

"Oh, honey, I can't imagine loving anyone as much as I love you." He pulled her into his arms. "What do you say, Marisa? Take a chance on a singing cowboy who wants to sing to you for the rest of his life?"

"Yes." The single word whispered out of her. "Oh, Mac, I want you to sing to me every night for the rest of my life. I want you to sing to our babies. I want…" She didn't finish, for his mouth cast down on hers in a tender kiss that spoke to her heart, to her very soul.

When the kiss ended, he didn't let her go. He looked into her eyes and smiled. "Tell me again that you're going to marry me."

"I'm going to marry you," she said and laughed as a blossom of warmth opened up in her chest. "Oh, Mac, I'm going to marry you and love you forever."

"This is a wonderful day for Big Cass," he said.

She looked at him in confusion. "Why is that?"

"All she ever wanted for her lost boys was that they would all find love. I was the last cowboy standing alone and unhappy, but now we've all found what Cass wanted most for us and that's love."

As his lips claimed hers once again she knew she'd found her home. If a darkness inside her began to encroach she knew with certainty that Mac would guide her back to the light.

She also knew with certainty that Mac was her forever man and her future with him would be one of laughter and sweet music and love.

Epilogue

The Holiday barn had once again been transformed, this time for a Christmas celebration for all the men who worked on the ranch. The evergreen tree chosen for its beauty reached halfway to the tall ceiling and was covered with red-and-silver ribbons and ornaments. The little white lights blinked off and on as if cheerfully winking at everyone.

The air was redolent with the scents of turkey and baked ham, of cinnamon-laced sweet potatoes and spiced apples. Cookie had made sure there was also stuffing, gravy, mac and cheese, and a dozen pies to feed all the ranch hands and their families.

Mac and Marisa stood near the tree where dozens of gaily wrapped presents were stacked up. The gifts weren't for the cowboys, who had seen their gifts in their paychecks with Christmas bonuses. Cassie always made sure the children of the cowboys had gifts beneath the tree.

Holiday music played from a speaker overhead, battling with the chatter and laughter of all the people inside the barn. Marisa leaned toward him. "Does she always wear something like that on her head?" she asked and gestured to a woman across the barn.

Mac couldn't help laughing. The woman in question was Tony Nakni's wife's grandmother, Halena. She was famous in town for her unusual and mostly over-the-top hats. Tonight she wore one that consisted of a six-to-eight-inch purple Christmas tree. It twinkled with multicolored lights and had little silver-and-gold ornaments all over it.

"Yes, just wait until you see her Easter hat," Mac replied. Marisa laughed and the sound of it was better than any Christmas carol that might ring in the air.

Mac jingled his car keys nervously in the pocket of his pants. He was definitely feeling more than a little bit anxious tonight. While he and Marisa had proclaimed their love to each other and he'd asked her to marry him, nothing official had really happened.

Tonight, he intended to make the engagement official. He had a beautiful engagement ring nestled in a box next to his car keys and he intended to drop to one knee in front of all of their friends before the night was over. Despite all the love they had shared since her captor had been locked up and they'd come back together, he was ridiculously nervous that she might tell him no. He was afraid the dream he'd been living was just too good to be true.

"Hey, Dusty," Mac greeted his friend as he approached with his very pregnant wife, Tricia. "Trish, you look beautiful as always," he added.

"Horse manure," she replied with a laugh. "I look like a whale."

"No, really. You look positively beautiful," Marisa said.

"Thanks, Marisa." Tricia offered her a shy smile. "Maybe you'd be open to coming over and having a cup of coffee with me some time."

Marisa hesitated only a minute. "I would like that," she replied.

Mac was so proud of Marisa. Even though she would suffer for years to come with the residual effects of the horrors visited upon her by Joe Mills, she was taking baby steps to make new friends.

Tony and his wife, Mary, joined them. "Earlier we were admiring Halena's hat," Mac said.

Mary rolled her eyes and then cast a fond gaze across the room to where Halena was speaking with Dillon and Cassie. "What can I say, she's a kook, but she's my kook."

"Our kook," Tony added with a loving look at his wife.

For the next few minutes, the four of them visited and then the dinner bell rang and people began to line up at the buffet.

Plates were filled and seats were found at the various tablecloth-covered picnic tables. Cassie said a short prayer. "Now is the time not to look backward, but rather to look forward and focus on the future," she continued. "Some of the faces here are different, with many of you new to the ranch. But when you sign up to be a Holiday Ranch cowboy, you automatically become part of a family. Cheers to all of you! Now let's eat."

And eat they did. Mac finally called it good after having not one but two pieces of Cookie's apple pie, although he whispered to Marisa that the pie didn't hold a candle to hers.

At the end of the meal, Mac excused himself from the table and went to where Cassie and Dillon sat. By the time he told Cassie what he intended to do, her eyes twinkled brightly.

"What was that all about?" Marisa asked when he returned to the table.

"Nothing important," he replied.

When Cassie finally stood and tinged the side of her glass with her knife to quiet everyone down, Mac's nerves went wild inside him.

"I am going to turn things over for a few moments to Mac." She smiled at him. "Mac, you now have the floor."

Mac stood, his heart banging an unsteady rhythm in his chest. If he was wrong about Marisa's love for him, then he was about to make a fool of himself in front of all the people he cared about. He turned to gaze at Marisa, who smiled up at him in confusion. Clad in a red sequined sweater that was a perfect complement for her black hair and creamy complexion, she looked as beautiful as he'd ever seen her.

The room fell silent, and as Mac gazed into Marisa's eyes, all his nerves calmed. "Marisa, I know I've told you how much I love you, but tonight I thought I would show you." He fell to one knee and everyone erupted with whoops and hollers.

"Mac…what are you doing?" Marisa said.

He smiled at her. The room quieted again and Mac took the ring box out of his pocket. "Marisa, I wanted to make it official." He opened the box to display the princess-cut diamond ring. "Will you marry me?"

"Yes, of course I will," she replied, half laughing and half crying. He slid the ring on her finger and then pulled her up and into his arms. Once again, the room exploded with cheers.

He took her lips in a kiss that held all his love, and he tasted her love for him. "Please carry on," he said to everyone once the kiss ended.

After dinner, he and Marisa and Dusty and Tricia visited with two of the new men. Tucker had come solo to the celebration, having broken up with his girlfriend a few weeks before. Brad Adams wasn't dating anyone and lamented the fact that he'd come alone.

"Congratulations to both of you," Tucker said.

"Thanks," Mac replied.

"Let me see that ring," Tricia said. Marisa held out her hand. "Oh, Mac, you did good."

Dusty turned to the two new cowboys. "You know Mac was the last cowboy standing when it came to finding his perfect woman. Now that he and Marisa are together, all of us original Holiday cowboys are happily married or engaged. Now we need to start working on you all finding the perfect women for you."

"Oh no, watch out for Dusty the matchmaker," Mac said with a laugh.

"Big Cass would want me to help these guys," Dusty replied.

Mac took hold of Marisa's hand as memories of Big Cass filled his head. She had taken a bunch of kids from unhappy backgrounds and welcomed them into her home…into her heart.

She would be happy that eleven boys had found love and happiness. He squeezed Marisa's hand and his heart swelled with happiness and love.

He knew their love was going to last a lifetime. As Cassie had said, it was time to start looking forward, and Mac couldn't wait to spend his future with Marisa.

* * * * *

*Don't forget previous titles in the
Cowboys of Holiday Ranch series:*

The Cowboy's Targeted Bride
Cowboy's Vow to Protect
Cowboy Defender
Guardian Cowboy
Sheltered by the Cowboy
Killer Cowboy

*Available now from
Harlequin Romantic Suspense!*

#2163 COLTON 911: UNDER SUSPICION
Colton 911: Chicago • by Bonnie Vanak

Widowed cop Harry Cartwright is investigating the death of a Colton patriarch, and all signs point to Sara Sandoval—the man's long-lost daughter. But Harry isn't sure if his feelings are clouding his judgment—until the real killer makes Sara a target...

#2164 PROVING COLTON'S INNOCENCE
The Coltons of Grave Gulch • by Lara Lacombe

Baldwin Bowe is a ghost bounty hunter who is determined to bring his brother to justice. But his professional resolve is tested when he falls for Jillian Colton, the woman his brother is bent on hurting.

#2165 TEXAS RANCHER'S HIDDEN DANGER
by Karen Whiddon

On the run from a serial killer client, therapist Amelia Ferguson tries to disappear in Getaway, Texas, going to work on single dad Ted Sanders's ranch. Something about the town and the handsome rancher appeal to her, but can their developing relationship survive a serial killer set on revenge?

#2166 HIS TO DEFEND
by Sharon C. Cooper

Amina Kelly may be divorced, but she wouldn't want her ex dead. When her ex is killed on duty, Maxwell Layton comes back into her life—and the passion between them is just as strong as ever. Now they have to fix their past mistakes—while dodging someone intent on making sure Amina doesn't get out alive...

SPECIAL EXCERPT FROM

(H) HARLEQUIN

ROMANTIC SUSPENSE

*Amina Kelly may be divorced, but she wouldn't
want her ex dead. When her ex is killed on duty,
Maxwell Layton comes back into her life—and the
passion between them is just as strong as ever. Now they
have to fix their past mistakes—while dodging someone
intent on making sure Amina doesn't get out alive…*

Read on for a sneak preview of
His to Defend,
the latest thrilling romance from Sharon C. Cooper!

"All of that's true and I hate this has happened to you,"
Maxwell said. "But you've forgotten one important fact.
You weren't harmed. At least not physically. Everything
in that house can be replaced."

"That might be true, but—"

"But you—" he kissed the side of her forehead
"—sweetheart, you're irreplaceable, and I'm glad you
weren't hurt. Now, *that*? That would've made the evening
a helluva lot worse. Because if that had happened, I
would be out for blood. We wouldn't be sitting here
together because I'd be out hunting that bastard. Instead,
we have others looking into the situation while you and I
are getting ready to try to salvage our date. So how about
we start by enjoying an excellent meal?"

After a long beat of silence, Amina sighed dramatically and leaned back to look up at him. A slow smile tugged the corners of her lips. "Well, when you put it that way, I guess I should pick a restaurant, huh?"

He grinned and handed her the menus. "Yes, and I'll take the bags upstairs, then change clothes. When I come back down, we can order." He stood and headed for the stairs again but stopped when she called him. "Yeah?"

"Thanks for coming to the house. It meant a lot to have you there with me even though I know it was the last place you wanted to be."

He studied her for a moment. "That might've been the case at first, but I want to be wherever you are, Amina. And I'll always be here, there or wherever for you. Remember that."

Don't miss
His to Defend *by Sharon C. Cooper,*
available January 2022 wherever
Harlequin Romantic Suspense
books and ebooks are sold.

Harlequin.com

Love Harlequin romance?

DISCOVER.

Be the first to find out about promotions,
news and exclusive content!

 Facebook.com/HarlequinBooks

 Twitter.com/HarlequinBooks

 Instagram.com/HarlequinBooks

 Pinterest.com/HarlequinBooks

 YouTube.com/HarlequinBooks

ReaderService.com

EXPLORE.

Sign up for the Harlequin e-newsletter and
download a free book from any series at
TryHarlequin.com

CONNECT.

Join our Harlequin community to
share your thoughts and connect
with other romance readers!
Facebook.com/groups/HarlequinConnection

HARLEQUIN

Heartfelt or thrilling, passionate or uplifting—Harlequin is more than just happily-ever-after.

With twelve different series to choose from and new books available every month, you are sure to find stories that will move you, uplift you, inspire and delight you.